NORTHERN RESCUE

LARGE PRINT

SHANA GRAY

Northern Rescue
Copyright © 2024 Shana Gray
First electronic publication May 17, 2022
Second electronic publication January 2023
First paperback publication April 2024
Edited by Paula Eykelhof
eBook ISBN: 978-0-9948635-5-3
Paperback: 978-1-7383480-1-5
Large Print Paperback: 978-1-7383480-6-0

Sign up for Shana's Newsletter":
http://www.shanagray.com/

ACKNOWLEDGMENTS

The idea for Northern Rescue came after speaking with my author friend Tee O'Fallon. We had a good gab, with martinis of course, via Zoom and plotted the book out. Rhian Cahill was also an amazing supporter offering up her wisdom, as she always does. Special *woofs* to my dog walker Dawn, who walks Hiro with his pals, and for providing some weird pups traits. To Kathleen Gazey for her knowledge of the northern forests. And to Paula Eykelhof for editing Northern Rescue, and being a friend.

~

Without rescue shelters many creatures in need of help and comfort would be lost - whether fur, scales, hair, wings, hooves. I can't fathom the need for rescues but grateful for them helping these sweet creatures.

*In particular, I'd like to mention Golden Rescue Canada, and their 30+ years of believing in second chances. I became a volunteer three years ago and where I found my Hiro, he's simply wonderful. GR rescues golden retrievers across Canada and overseas until the ban. Without them, many goldens would not find their fur-ever homes. **Northern Rescue** is dedicated to GR and it's many volunteers and supporters.*

1

I've always been one to take a challenge head-on. You know, jump right in with both feet and let whatever happens, happen—all those cliches. Maybe I'm a little too impetuous by nature. But *c'est la vie*. I look for the positive in most areas of life and I was optimistic there'd be one in this situation, too. There *had* to be.

I never worried about a safety net. Perhaps that was thanks to my privileged upbringing. I appreciated where I came from and was determined to do my best to make a difference. Somehow.

And that's how I ended up in Churchill, Manitoba, the land of polar bears, with a pack of homeless dogs *and* in the middle of winter.

Eleven dogs waiting for me in the middle of

nowhere. Waiting for me to fly them to their forever homes.

I'd been told there were only five. The pilot was expecting five. I could rehome five, but eleven?

Rebecca Gardner, you hate winter. Hate cold. What are you doing here? I snorted, and realized my nostrils were stuck together it was so cold.

I'm saving dogs! I told myself.

The handoff of the dogs at the small terminal was relatively easy. I shoved the envelope I was given into the front of my coat and hoped it wouldn't fall out on the way to the plane.

The frigid temperature had almost numbed my fingers. I didn't need to be told I should've dressed more appropriately for the conditions. I'd never been north before, so hadn't experienced bitter cold. Not to mention I'd been more focused on the details of saving the dogs than my own comfort.

Maybe there was even a little bit of wanting to look good for the pilot I'd hired. Barrett Kingston was dangerously attractive with a wide smile and even white teeth behind his dark mustache and beard. I was especially caught by his eyes. Sparkling blue, ringed with dark lashes and arched brows. Shaggy hair that fell over his forehead. The type of man I rarely came across in my world.

Rugged. Yes, that was what I'd call him.

My skinny jeans, knee-high spike-heeled boots, fitted hip length pea jacket and fingerless gloves might be fine for wintry city streets but definitely not for this arctic weather. My hair whipped around my head and would be a complete rat's nest by the end of the day.

What I wouldn't give for a parka, hat, gloves and -100 degrees rated boots! I clenched my hands around the leashes, barely feeling them.

Eleven! Eleven dogs!

There was no way I'd leave any of them here. Where would they go? What would happen to them? Who would care for them? My heart ached for these poor lonely souls. They'd been shuffled around to foster homes after the shelter caught fire. They needed stability, love and permanent homes. Caring homes.

It was my job to make that happen.

I pulled on the leashes, trying to keep them in hand, and looked across the tarmac at Barrett's plane. How was I going to explain this to him? I sensed a hesitancy in him and wasn't sure why, I didn't want to pry so I worked my magic on him. Finally, he succumbed to my persuasion and accept the job offer. And, I was glad he had.

The husky leaned into his collar, stepping up the pace, and the other dogs fell into the run with him, except the little ones. They were pulled behind, doing their best to keep up with their little legs.

I was yanked forward and nearly pulled off my feet. Imagine – me, sophisticated city girl, face planted and dragged along by a pack of dogs. Instead, I ran in mini-steps behind them, desperate to keep my footing. Cursing my stiletto boots.

"Whoa, whoa, dogs!" I shouted. Clearly, they had no understanding of voice commands.

I clutched all the leashes, desperate not to let any of them get away. I didn't want to think what a debacle that would be, chasing almost a dozen runaway dogs around the small airport.

"Easy now!" I ordered through gritted teeth, positive the dogs had selective hearing.

The big dogs were powerful engines, drawing everyone along behind them. The leashes got all tangled and it was as if all the pups blended into one massive mess.

The Great Pyrenees and Golden Retriever lurched on their leashes, which fired up the husky. He let out a howl and leaned into his collar, yanking the bunch along, again almost jerking me off my treacherous and stupid heels. I scrambled for footing, clutching the leashes like a lifeline as I was hauled across the pavement, feet flying.

The image of a running Phoebe from *Friends* flashed through my mind. I couldn't help myself and started to laugh, which was totally the wrong thing to do when I was flailing along behind the pack of dogs like an idiot.

"Dogs. Stop! Heel, heel, heel," I yelled behind a bubble of laughter. "Pleeeease." I begged them to listen to me and knew I was in a losing battle. "Oh, doggies, heel."

If Tess, my friend waiting to pick me up at our airport a couple of hours north of Toronto, could see me now, she wouldn't believe it and would've caught the whole scenario on video and posted it on social media. I knew the visual of an inappropriately dressed woman, handling a pack of dogs, running across an airport tarmac in the middle of winter wasn't something you saw every day.

Gasping for breath, I managed to slow the unruly pups and steer them in the direction of the waiting plane. My arms and shoulders ached.

Finally, they settled to a walk, still pretty high-octane, but at least I had some semblance of control now. My heart pounded from exertion, and worry they'd get away from me. I simply couldn't handle the thought of the dogs getting loose and having to herd them back together.

Their chorus of barks echoed across the tarmac and runway, offering perfect acoustics.

They just seemed so damn happy. Tails wagged

and tongues lolled. Did they know a better life lay ahead for them?

Steering them in the general direction of the plane was like turning a big ship. Slow and arduous, but eventually we were all beelining it toward Barrett. Not for the first time I was concerned we wouldn't all fit in the plane. I refused to leave any of them behind.

Barrett walked around the nose of the plane. He looked in my direction as I bore down on him with all the dogs. The expression on his face said it all. Surprise. Disbelief. Concern.

A scrawny little pooch escaped, her thin leash slipping through my fingers, and she took off like a bullet, which set the other dogs in an uproar. The bigger ones yanked against their leashes and once again, I found myself flailing along behind them.

"Barrett!" I screamed. "Grab her!"

The little one headed right for Barrett. He crouched with his arms out like a bat catcher, maneuvering himself into her path. She leapt into his arms and started licking his face. He wrapped both arms around her and, damn it, I could imagine how strong and safe she felt being held by him.

"Hold on to her," I gasped as the lot of us came to a rambunctious halt in front of Barrett and his plane.

He stared at me for a second, then he looked at

the dogs. I couldn't tell what he was thinking and his shocked expression slid into an unreadable one. I was worried.

"You said only five." He struggled with the little lady wriggling in his grasp and licking his face. He chuckled and I smiled as relief rushed through me.

I clutched the leashes tighter to avoid any more potential escapes.

"I know. I was told five." I rushed my words and shrugged, keeping my voice light, hoping I sounded optimistic and like we could absolutely handle the extra pups. "Look at all these happy faces. We simply can't leave them behind."

I figured that maybe if I used "we" rather than "I," he'd feel more connected to the dogs.

I waited and watched him gazing at the pack. Would he make a fuss and tell me I couldn't bring them all? I shifted, my feet growing colder, as his silence drew out.

"The poor things have nowhere to go since the shelter burned and there aren't enough fosters in the area." I didn't have to feign sadness; it was etched my voice.

I saw the muscle in his jaw flex.

I waited. If I could've crossed my fingers, I would have.

The dog he had in his arms had snuggled into him and he was petting her. I wasn't sure he realized what he was doing as I watched his fingers twirl her ears.

He sighed. "Not sure how we're supposed to fit them all on the plane, but…"

"Well, we can put them in the back and block them from coming forward so they won't bother you while you're flying. I'll do my best to keep control of them. I promise." I held my breath. What was he going to say?

He shook his head and my heart sank. "I don't know what I've got myself into with this fiasco. We've gone from five dogs, to what?" he mumbled and quickly counted the pack of love-hungry pups. "Eleven. Eleven dogs."

"I know, I know. I'll pay you extra. But please, I can't leave any behind. I just can't." My eyes prickled and I blinked back the threatening tears. He was going to be a grump about it and I couldn't bear the thought that he might refuse to take some of the dogs.

"Here, I can't finish my preflight check with her licking my face." He put the dog down gently and handed me the little ragamuffin's leash. Ours fingers brushed and tingles ran up my arm. A rush of attraction to him washed over me. We'd talked a lot in the previous weeks via Zoom and cell, and it wasn't hard to fall under his bad boy spell. I blinked and looked up at him; our eyes met and lingered and for the briefest moment I forgot about the dogs. My tongue suddenly thick in my mouth, there was no use trying to form words.

He didn't move away from me until a little whine made him look down at the pup he'd been holding.

Rags, as I thought of her now, stared up at Barrett, her eyes big, sad, her little body shivering. She lifted a paw.

He leaned down and picked her up. "Aw, shit," was all he said and then he opened the door, putting her inside. "We'll load 'em up after I finish checking the plane."

"Oh, thank you, thank you," I blurted, perhaps a bit too enthusiastically.

The urge to leap into his arms and kiss him all over was powerful, and I was glad I had a handful of leashes keeping me grounded.

So this tough guy had a soft side after all.

2

"Okay, let's get on board." He glanced up at the sky. "Time to get cracking."

I didn't like the way he furrowed his brows and looked at the pack of dogs.

"Is something wrong?" I asked and peered at the graying sky. It was starting to get dark.

He shook his head. "No, just hoping we manage with them all."

"Thank you so much for being so understanding. Like I said, I'm happy to pay more for this inconvenience. I really had no idea there'd be more dogs."

He nodded. "Yeah, well there's not much we can do about it now. It's not like we're going to leave them behind. We should hurry. I'm not liking the look of the sky."

He stuck his hands on his hips and glanced around. I did, too. This was a very remote place, I imagined like tundra, and really quite beautiful in its own rather desolate way.

"Should the big ones go in first or the little ones?" he asked.

I shrugged my shoulders. "Well, maybe the big ones so they can find a place and the little ones can fit themselves in to the empty spaces," I suggested.

"Okay. Come on, big boy." Barrett took the leash of the Great Pyrenees and got him aboard, followed by the retriever, labs, husky and shepherd. He handled them calmly and with no reluctance. I was pleased the dogs didn't give him any resistance and settled into their assigned places.

"Okay, now the others."

A couple of the beagles bumped into the back of my legs, knocking out my knees. I stumbled, and started to fall. My heel caught in a crack and I was gone, crashing over.

I yelped. This was not going to be pretty and I braced myself for a hard landing, eyes squeezed shut. Strong hands grabbed me. The pups got all excited and jumped around our feet, tangling us up in their leashes.

He wrapped his arms, firm and strong, around my waist and we pressed together, chest to chest, hip to hip. I looked up and ours eyes met, mirth reflecting in his. Wasn't this a scenario from *101 Dal-matians*?

I gasped, struck by a powerful wave of arousal. It was the last thing I'd expected. Part of me was horrified by my clumsiness – and the other quite happy to wind up in his arms.

He was my savior. The dogs' savior. And words fled when I looked into his eyes.

Finally I was able to mutter. "Um, sorry about that." My voice sounded like a frog croaking and I pinched back a grimace.

Our eyes met. His, a sea-blue, held mine and I saw the briefest flicker of ... something. My stomach clenched and I lowered my eyes. I wasn't sure what kind of reaction I'd expected from him. If any. But I certainly hadn't expected *my* response to our sudden closeness.

We untangled ourselves in silence and I was dying to know what he was thinking.

"I guess we're going to have to expect that kind of chaos for the next few hours," I murmured. He gave me the briefest of smiles.

He was deep, this man. And I was intrigued as I watched him help the dogs into the plane

"Up you go, kids. Let's go for a car ride."

I laughed welcoming his spark of humor. "Car ride? Most dogs loved car rides. Come on, doggies, let's go for a car ride."

A few perked their ears and barked, obviously accustomed to the word. We loaded the beagles, shepherd, golden, the mystery breeds; they juggled for space and some settled down, while others stood and panted, tongues out, eyes concerned.

My eye prickled with the threat of tears. What had these pooches gone through? I refused to think of them as poor pups. Instead, I considered them lucky pups. They were getting another chance. I fully believed in *adopt, don't shop*, and would do my best to find them all loving homes.

"Okay, only these little guys left." He scooped the small dogs into his arms and gently placed them inside. "Okay, now you."

I took his hand and did my best to board the plane as gracefully as possible. Which was a feat in the skinny jeans and stiletto boots. Finally, I slid into the copilot seat and he closed the door. I watched him walk around the plane and then climb into the pilot seat with ease.

"Looks like we got them all packed in." Barrett adjusted himself in the seat.

He smiled and for a beat the heat between us felt like setting a match to a sheet of paper. Was I imagining things or was something going on? Something between us? I couldn't deny the flutter deep inside whenever he looked at me, especially after our entanglement moments before.

"Yes, they are."

I was glad we'd had conversations both by phone and video prior to meeting in person. I thought I was ready to be in close proximity to a stranger. But, I hadn't expected this magnetism.

I needed to distance myself. Nothing could happen between us, right? He was like a mountain man, wilderness was his life and I had my ... what? City life? The buzz and hustle of the life I was born into?

I zoned out while he began the plane take-off process.

I'd totally deviated from family expectations after completing uni. I wanted to make my own way in life and not be stuck fulfilling plans laid out since before I was even born. Of course, this made me a rebel, and there'd been loads of fights about it. But I stood my ground. My brother was the one that stuck to the family path, which made it easier for me to push back. The thought of being drawn into world charity events and foundation galas and champagne socials made me want to eat glass. I definitely didn't discount the value of them, I just felt there was something ...more.

Something I needed to do.

When news came to me, via a convoluted network of connections, about an animal rescue/shelter fire, rescue dogs being fostered and needing permanent homes, I knew it was a calling. It also gave me the chance to escape, vanish from the family radar for a little while, and the only person who knew my rescue plans was Tess. My best friend.

My parents were old school, and I'd dodged a bullet when they tried to push an engagement. Honestly, in this day and age, an arranged marriage? For a thirty-one year old? They'd threatened to cut me off. The more I pushed back, the more they threatened. And I almost caved. My prospective fiancé was also heavy-handed, which caused an uproar when I told my parents it totally wasn't going to happen! I dated, but always with the intention that I wouldn't be trapped into a relationship that was not of my choosing.

And, then this rescue opportunity presented itself and I wasn't going to let it pass me by. Among other things, it was an escape from the marital pressures. I had to do this now, while I still had access to my funds.

I sat back and let out a huff.

"What's up?" Barrett asked.

"Oh, nothing." I wasn't about to burden him with my ridiculous problems.

The dogs were restless. "I'm not sure if I should go back and take their leashes off. What you think?" I asked.

He twisted in his seat and looked back. The aura

he gave off with that simple movement was enough to make my mouth go dry. I could only imagine the strength and power that his leather jacket hid from me. We were everything opposite. I highly doubted either of us could adapt to the other's world.

"I don't really know, to be honest. I suppose it's best to take them off, because you don't want them getting all knotted up and tangled back there. When we land, we'll have to be careful none of them escape without a leash or collar."

I nodded.

"You haven't forgotten that we have to make a stop on the way down?" he reminded me.

I shook my head. "No, I remember. It'll just be quick, right?"

"That's the plan. A quick refuel and on our way. I want to beat this weather."

"Okay, then." I climbed between the two seats into the back and was immediately at the bottom of a joyous, happy, dog pile. They barked and whined, their tails wagged and most of them were licking my face and hands, making it nearly impossible to move.

I laughed under the happy dogs. I was doing something good here. Selfless and caring. What I'd yearned to do for such a long time. I embraced the dogs as they tumbled around me, tears filled my eyes and I snapped off their leashes. I wasn't sad, I was ecstatic and began to laugh. I was getting smothered in puppy love, and I couldn't have been happier.

Barrett chuckled, and I smiled at him through the wall of warm dog bodies.

"I think I may need some help getting out from under here." I laughed.

"You just might."

He reached back and I took his extended hand, using it as leverage to extract myself and clamber back into my seat.

"Whew. Thanks." He didn't let go of my hand and I let my fingers linger in his. "I'm glad we fit them all in," I said as I got myself back in the seat, glad I'd put a few bags of dog food and an overnight bag for me in the cargo behind the seats.

"Yep, we did," he said.

"Hopefully there aren't any accidents or puking. If that happens, I'll clean it up."

"Don't worry about it now. Do up your seatbelt." I nodded and reached for the belt, fumbling to find it. "Here, let me." He leaned over, pulled the seatbelt out, then reached between my legs for another buckle, his arms brushing my inner thigh. I gasped and my eyes widened. Another powerful rush of hormones took me by surprise.

He glanced at me with an unfathomable look

and then expertly snapped the seat buckles. He cleared his throat. Had he felt the same thing?

Moments later, we were on the runway and I fixed my eyes out the window as we picked up speed and took off. The husky decided it was the perfect time to let out a howl. The other dogs joined in.

"And we're off," I said.

I wasn't entirely sure how Barrett felt about dogs. He didn't gush over them, or push them away. He just accepted them. The little one on his lap seemed very comfortable. I realized it would have bothered with me if he didn't like dogs.

I looked up from the dog in his lap and was startled when we made eye contact.

He was grinning at me and damned if a bout of nervous butterflies didn't beat around in my belly. I swear I moaned. Thank God for the engine noise drowning me out.

He turned back to flying while my mind decided it was going on a trip of its own and ran away with some crazy thinking.

Us, together. Us, as a couple? Us.

We barely knew each other. I shook my head. Plus, our lives were different. He lived up here in the boonies, while I lived in the city, so this was stupid thinking. Boy did need sleep. I'd been on the go for ages.

I rested me head back and looked out the window. The vast expanse of wilderness below took my breath away, as did the man next to me. But, anyhoo...being out of the concrete jungle, away from the demands of my family, was wonderfully freeing.

I sighed as a wave of warmth spread through my body. My mind was unencumbered from all the worries, pressures, deadlines and concerns waiting for me when I got home. I couldn't pin down exactly how I was feeling, but I felt so damn good, I could've floated away, weightless and free.

I wondered if Barrett would run away. We could go...anywhere? He had the plane and I had the cash. Recipe for success.

I glanced at him. He was focused on flying—as he should be. On the flight north we'd been fairly quiet and I'd occupied myself on my laptop. We'd chatted a bit, and our silences were, well...comfortable. Barrett had a depth to him that intrigued me and he was even more gorgeous in person. I thought back to our Zoom conversations. They'd been succinct, but I was sure I'd detected an underlying tone of interest from him. Maybe it was just interest in this strange flight he'd agreed to. My Angel Flight to rescue all these wonderful pups.

Live cargo, as in dogs, wasn't really his thing.

He'd told me his base customers were tourists, business execs, a few medical evacs and, on the odd occasion, exploration companies or businesses that needed to move their people up and around the north.

I was curious about his background. Could his basic clientele be enough to keep him in the air? But before I had a chance to wonder about it anymore, I glanced out the window—and saw that the sky had suddenly darkened.

3

I felt an energy coming from Barrett that hadn't been there before and sensed that something bad was going to happen. I knew we were racing against time and weather. I looked out my window again and pulled my lower lip between my teeth. The sky had darkened even more. I swallowed, and every cell in my body wanted to ask him if we were going to be okay.

The pups in my lap squirmed and let out a little mewl. I glanced down at him and realized I'd been gripping him a bit too tight. His big, soft, brown eyes looked up at me through his fluff of bangs.

I leaned down and kissed him on the head.

"I'm sorry, buddy." My words were soft and low against his furry neck.

The warmth of his little body comforted my

sudden anxiety. I still found it hard to believe I was in the air with a man I'd only just met in person, and a pack of dogs. Six months ago, if you'd asked me what I'd be doing, this certainly wasn't it.

But here I was, and while I felt terrified to be flying, I was also thrilled to be on the first of (hopefully) many Angel Flights. The dogs had kept my mind occupied and my fear of flying at bay. Until now.

"You okay?" Barrett asked.

His question surprised me. He'd been so focused on flying.

"Why do you ask?"

"You're acting weird," was all he said. Blunt.

"I don't think I am. But I'm getting a vibe off you like something's wrong."

He sighed. "Nothing's wrong. Just watching the weather."

I nodded, still determined not to voice my worry. Keeping the dogs calm was a good way to avoid thinking about the weather. As long as my anxiety didn't transfer to them...

The dogs were finally settling in the back of the plane, I had one at my feet and he warmed my legs. The two on my lap kept me toasty. I just wanted to hug all the dogs and reassure them that everything would be fine.

The dogs and I fell into a trancelike state, the

drone of the engines a soothing white noise, and I felt my eyes droop. Maybe I could catch a few winks.

The plane lurched and I sat bolt upright.

Dogs yipped in surprise and the cabin filled with their chorus of barks. I gasped, flinging out my hands to steady myself. One hand gripped Barrett's muscular forearm and the other was planted against the window.

"What was that?" I yelped and kept my eyes closed.

"Just a bit of turbulence. I warned you about it. No need to worry." The calm tone of his voice did little to comfort me. "You can open your eyes now."

I squinted through one eye and kept the other closed.

He was smiling, which I had to admit helped ease my angst. I highly doubted he'd be smiling if we were about to crash.

I nodded and opened my other eye. "O-okay. I hope it doesn't happen again."

"It might, so be prepared."

"W-why?"

He pointed out the window. "The weather's coming in faster than forecast. Plus we need to set down for gas soon."

I was alarmed. "We're running out of gas?"

"We will if we don't refuel," was all he told me.

I fell silent, going over in my head that we could

run out of gas. I knew we had to stop, and now it seemed like something of an emergency.

I petted the dogs jumbled on my lap, I didn't mind that they were heavy and I was practically squished, my thoughts shifted to them. I tried to put the mechanics of flying and the need for gas out of my mind--I'd leave it to the expert--and refocus on the warm bodies. That I could do. It was hard giving all of them the attention they wanted and once we were off the plane, I'd hug them all.

Another dog crawled into my lap; I wrapped my arms around the bunch of them. He wasn't really a lap dog, but under current circumstances I welcomed the warm, large body to the pile. I clutched the dogs tight, positive I could hear their hearts beating. I guessed they didn't like flying either.

The variety of dogs surprised me, small to extra-large. beagles, lab mixes, huskies, a shepherd, Golden Retriever, Great Pyrenees, a few other mixed breeds that were hard to determine, and of course the two little ladies. They touched my heart. Small, old, scruffy and in dire need of a bath. Poor things. Right now, they were cuddled up on Barrett's lap, and had worked their way under his coat.

I wish Tess had been able to come. I could've used the extra help with all these dogs. I'd told her no, I could manage and there probably wouldn't be enough room for her anyway. I was correct on that point.

She was to meet us when we landed. I regretted not texting her before we took off, asking her to bring a bigger vehicle, and that we were going to arrive late.

The plane bucked. I gasped, doing my best to keep calm, burying my face in the warm fur. Obviously, I wasn't a fan of flying, even on a big jet. Being on a much smaller plane somewhere over the vast and empty land below, covered in snow and ice and trees as far as the eye could see, was not comforting

Barrett didn't appear concerned. He handled the controls like the expert he was, but his expression had tightened a bit.

I wasn't sure if it was because he was concentrating or the fact that he had eleven dogs packed into his plane and we were surrounded by panting, small cries and the occasional howl. Or...the weather was worse than he'd told me.

I needed to stop overthinking and told myself if there was something to worry about, he'd tell me. Right?

No, he wouldn't.

I clutched the dogs tighter. We just had to get all these beautiful doggos safely on the ground so they could find their new homes.

The plane dropped, nose down, and it felt as if

we were weightless. Hovering in space. I was strapped in with a seatbelt, but the dogs weren't. And they all floated up and around us before the plane caught itself and the dogs tumbled down back on the seats. A riot of barking filled the cabin. The momentary peace and quiet had vanished. Maybe it was good we had to land.

Barrett chuckled. "That would've been a good photo op for you. Dogs suspended in air."

"I didn't like it, and I'm sure they didn't, either," I said matter of fatly.

Their panting, barking and carrying on drowned out the steady drone of the engines.

"There'll be more turbulence." Barrett stated matter-of-factly. "But don't worry, we'll be fine."

He had the perfect radio voice. Deep, calm and, of course, very sexy. I had to admit it did make me feel a little better.

"Is the bad weather catching up with us?" I looked out the window and the darkening smudge of clouds seemed closer.

"Yep." He glanced out and furrowed his eyebrows. He looked at me, I looked at him, and for a beat we stared at each other before he looked back at the controls.

"We knew this weather was coming and we were racing against time." There was an edge to his voice. I felt like he was reprimanding me.

"I'm sorry if I delayed us with the extra dogs." The urge to explain myself was strong.

He grunted as the plane jostled in the sky again.

"No, it's not you or the dogs." He was gently stroking the little old ladies curled up in his lap, and I smiled. "We're low on fuel and it'll set us back when we land to refuel. I just hope we're not snowed in by the time we get there. I'll have to be quick, and you'll need to keep the dogs in the plane. We won't have any time to spare if we want to beat this system. It does look like it's shifting." He tapped the radar screen on the console.

"Shifting?" I asked him, concerned, and twisted around to check the bank of clouds on the horizon. They were darker and closer than a few minutes ago. "Snow!" I shouted when a flurry whisked past the windows. "Do we really have to stop?" The vast expanse of snow-brushed trees below, with no airport or town in sight, was not the most comforting. "Surely there's extra gas in the tank. They always have a reserve built in, don't they?"

He chuckled and I felt a surge of anger that he could laugh in a situation like this.

"No extra in the tank. It's a necessary stop to ensure that we have enough fuel for your precious cargo to arrive safely."

"Precious cargo," I whispered and turned around to look at the dogs in the back.

Most of them were panting, and, of course the Pyr was drooling everywhere. "I really don't know why you're laughing. It's not funny," I blurted out.

"I never said it was."

"But you were laughing."

"Only at you." He smiled.

"Hmph. Well, if we crash and die, at least I won't have to clean up your leather seats." I found it difficult to hold onto my flash of anger. It was more that I felt stupid about my comment. Running out of gas...sheesh. My anger floated away on the flurries of snow surrounding the plane.

"No, you won't."

I stared out the window. I wanted to see if he was still grinning, but forced myself not to. His confidence eased my nerves so I could put everything in perspective. His quiet efficiency calmed me.

Somewhat.

A golden pushed his way to me through the tangle of legs and tails, and nudged my elbow. I looked down at him and his eyes bored right into me. Goldens sure could turn on the eyes when they wanted to.

His eyes, deep, brown, liquid and sorrowful, almost broke my heart. I lifted my elbow and he rested his chin on my thigh. "What a precious you are. What a hero. Such a gorgeous big boy."

"Why, thank you," Barrett said.

"What?" I looked at him and then realized he thought I was talking about him. "No, not you. The dog."

He laughed and I gave him a swat on the arm, and found myself joining in with a chuckle.

After that, we flew for a little while in silence. When the husky at the back let out a low, long yowl peppered with yips, I nearly jumped out of my skin. She was talkative and carried on a conversation with herself. The beagle decided to join in the chat with her and soon the cabin was filled with barks, cries, howls and whines.

"Shh, dogs. Quiet." I reached back trying to pet the closest ones, and they carried on with their canine opera. I had to wonder what tales they were telling each other, maybe explaining to each other how they'd ended up here. From somewhere to shelter to foster and now they were all on a plane. They had no clue what was happening and where they'd land. That was my responsibility. And I was determined they would all find loving homes.

"Sorry, it's hard to keep them quiet."

"It's fine. I don't blame them for being out of sorts." Barrett continued to stroke the little mutts in his lap and my chest tightened. Hopefully, these little old girls would go home with him. Would I have to sell him on the idea? Could I?

"Where are we stopping for gas?" I asked and

then giggled when a mixed breed came up and started licking my neck from behind.

He glanced over and smiled.

"I have a place."

"You have a place? Really? Out here in the middle of nowhere."

He raised his eyebrows and shrugged. "Why not?"

He didn't elaborate. I wanted to ask him more, like why he'd live so far away from everyone. Wasn't it lonely? I glanced out the window, seeing the smudge of trees through the falling snow. It looked so lost and forlorn with a wild beauty I had to admit was breathtaking. Still, I shivered and couldn't imagine being this isolated.

I wondered if he ever lived in the city and why he'd leave it? Could someone like me ever adapt to wilderness life?

I supposed it didn't matter, because neither of us would need to find out. I gave a quick glance at him...and a brief tightening in my chest made me wonder.

A whimper came from his lap. One of the little ladies was dreaming.

I watched her twitch and my heart broke again. All these sweet, homeless pups. I simply couldn't imagine what they'd gone through before now. It was far too painful. Tears filled my eyes as I reached over to run my fingers down her nose. She looked up at me with half-closed eyes when I gently twirled her ears. She was shivering. "I wish I'd brought more blankets. Could've wrapped her up to keep her warm."

"It is hard to see these poor animals go through this." Barrett said and the other little pup on his lap looked up at him. Her ears perked.

"She likes your voice," I said with a smile.

He patted her gently, and our fingers brushed. A spark, hot and electric, from his touch jolted up my arm. I glanced at him to see if he'd felt it, too.

Our eyes met and we stared at each other until she gave a little whine. The other pup tucked into his coat made a yip of protest and then the two of them maneuvered themselves into a cozy ball with their faces tucked into his stomach.

He lifted his arms, looked down, then at me.

"They like you," I said.

"I guess they do." He lowered his arms and lifted his coat, so the dogs were covered by the warmth. He rested his hands on them, and the little dogs snuggled even closer. I watched the expression on his face as it softened. He gave a gentle smile.

Maybe he was a dog person, after all.

4

I watched the approaching clouds and glanced at Barrett. We'd been silent for the last little while. The dogs had settled down and I think we both figured, as they say, that we should let sleeping dogs lie.

He was stroking the dog's head poking out from under his coat. Her eyes were closed and if dogs could smile, I was pretty sure she was grinning from ear to ear. Watching him with the dogs out of the corner of my eye, I felt the strangest sensation tighten in my chest. I was beginning to see him in a new light. A gentler, softer light that changed him from the gruff, sorta grumpy guy, to a deeper, sensitive, intriguing man.

I liked this change.

I smiled and looked down at the jumble of paws,

wet noses and fluffy ears all around me. This had been absolutely the right thing to do. There was no question.

The plane jostled in the air once more. The dog behind me stirred and some of them stood up. I reached back hoping to calm them. And they all scrambled over of each other to reach my hand.

"It's okay baby, it's okay. You're doing fine. Bunch of sweet pups. We'll be on the ground soon," I crooned, my voice competing with the sound of the engines and the wind.

"I don't think they're doing too well," I said to Barrett.

He turned around to look and nodded. "Still, better than expected." He moved in his seat, and the two old ladies in his lap whined their displeasure. "I hope none of them have to relieve themselves."

I nodded. "Yes, I know. I think dogs are pretty good at holding it. But nerves and being in the plane could change that."

"Do you know a lot about dogs?"

"Enough I suppose. I hope anyway. I've done a lot of reading, and have volunteered with a rescue association. They specialize in rescuing Golden Retrievers, even some overseas."

"Then I think you're set," Barrett said.

I'd covered the floor and the seats in case someone had an accident. So far, so good. The interior was more posh than I'd expected, with its leather seats, and very clean. I was a little surprised he'd agreed to fly the dogs at all. In case of, you know, accidents.

I'd be sure to have his plane detailed for him. It hadn't been part of our agreement, but it was the right thing to do.

We hit a pocket of turbulence again and this time it was a little more violent. Dogs became restless and pushed their way toward us.

"You have to keep them back there," Barrett warned.

I twisted in my seat, not wanting to take off my seatbelt.

The big dogs trampled over the smaller ones, and it wasn't easy to keep them organized. I debated sitting in the back with them, but that would upset the ones clustered around me.

The big head of the Great Pyrenees hung over Barrett's shoulder, his tongue lolling as great streams of sticky drool pooled on his jacket. The husky started to talk, yip and howl again. It was almost ear-shattering. I was starting to feel relieved we had to make a stop.

A barking chorus filled the plane, and I looked at Barrett to see if he was upset. He gave no indication that he was annoyed. He continued to stroke the little ones in his lap. His attention was out the window.

"Do we have to go much farther? It seems to be getting a little rough," I said, trying to keep my voice steady.

"It is," he replied. "But we have to refuel. I don't like how quickly this front's coming in. We should be on the ground in about--" he checked his watch "--fifteen minutes. Like I said, we have to be quick or we'll be grounded."

I nodded. The sinking sensation in my stomach was hard to ignore. Were we in danger?

I had to trust this man that I'd just met in person.

Barrett Kingston. Bush pilot. A man I knew practically nothing about. And here I was, trusting him with my life. To fly me in a small plane, up to land of the midnight sun and back. Just the two of us. High in the skies, over snowy wilderness. To rescue a pack of homeless dogs.

"Do you think we'll be grounded? Will we be able to take off?" I asked, now getting even more alarmed. I licked my lips trying to read his expression.

His lips tightened and the muscle in his jaw tensed. Did that mean he was nervous? Worried?

I had to bite my tongue to keep from firing a bunch of questions at him and let him focus on flying the stupid plane, which continued to buck in the air.

He looked over, a flash of annoyance reflected in his eyes, and I couldn't contain myself. "What's upsetting you? I can see it on your face."

He shook his head.

"Come on, don't clam up. Be honest with me. Tell me what's going on." It was as if the whole mood in the plane changed. I felt my spine tingle.

"Definitely it's a challenge with all the dogs. And I understand rescuing them." He was still stroking the sleeping dogs in his lap. "We have to land and refuel, and I have to do a quick property check —

"Do we have time for that?" I was getting worried. He'd never said anything about it before.

"As long as you keep the dogs in the plane, we should do."

The snowflakes had thickened and it was becoming difficult to see.

"Oh, God, it's starting to snow." Dread soured my stomach. I took out my phone. No signal. I decided to distract myself by taking some photos in the plane. It would be good for promo.

"Don't worry. I can fly IFR."

"IFR?"

He glanced at me. "Instrument flight rating. It means I don't need to have visual contact with the ground. I can fly by the instruments."

My mouth made the shape of an O and I nodded.

We hit another pocket of turbulence and the dogs all rose in up again, as if they were weightless. I was snapping photos and caught images of them floating in the air. Their ears lifted and they all looked rather stunned to be hanging there. Thankfully, the plane righted itself smoothly and without a jolt. The dogs settled back into their spots. It would've been almost comical if we weren't in this situation.

"Well, that quieted them a bit," Barrett said with a smile on his face.

"Looks like it did. Maybe they should go weightless more often." I laughed, my nerves easing somewhat, and he joined me; A brief bit of comic relief in the middle of a worrying situation was always good.

"Do we land at an airport and then drive to your property?"

He shook his head. "No, I have a runway on site."

"Really? You do? What happens if it gets covered in snow or ice? Can we still land? Still take off?" So. Many. Questions.

"I have snow removal equipment, and as long as it isn't too deep, we'll be fine."

The snow was getting thicker outside the plane, and I had a feeling things might not be going as planned.

"Okay, beginning my descent."

I watched him handle the controls and his confidence relaxed my wayward thoughts.

We banked and flew out of the snow. I twisted in my seat to see how far behind we were leaving it. I imagined the clouds turning into a face like the sand in *The Mummy*, chasing us and gobbling up the plane.

The plane banked again, and I searched the ground below. As we circled around, I saw a long narrow cut in the forest below, close to what looked like a frozen lake.

Surely that wasn't the runway! I stared down at it. The sun peeked out from the clouds, and I pressed my hand to my mouth, thankful for the brightness. Maybe it would be okay, after all.

The trees rose up fast as we descended. I gripped the dogs in my lap and desperately searched for the runway as we skimmed the treetops.

Then the sun disappeared, and it was as if darkness descended. The snow had caught up to us and I could barely see the trees anymore.

I looked at Barrett.

He was focused, tense, and I closed my eyes. Hoping for the best but bracing for the worst.

"Damn," he muttered under his breath and the plane dipped again. "Hang on."

Oh, Lord!

5

"I hope you know what you're doing!" I thought it but didn't say it, tucking my chin into the collar of my coat and squinted. Not really wanting to see how close we were to the trees.

Tall, lanky pines, spruce, and wintry skeletons of leafless trees reached up as if to grab us as we zipped over top of them. They vanished behind us and a narrow strip devoid of trees appeared through the flurries. Was that the runway? It was just a track carved out of the surrounding forest with snow slithering along its length.

I held my breath when we touched down with a bump and the plane raced along the runway, slowly coming to a halt before a building I guessed was a hangar.

I let out a shaky breath. We'd survived the landing.

Barrett did whatever he had to do with the controls and then turned to me. "Okay," he said. "You wait here. Don't let the dogs out and I'll finish quick as I can."

The dogs were restless now that we'd landed, noses pressed to the windows and tails wagging. I wondered if they needed to go out for a pee. They were panting and a couple were crying.

"Oh, sweeties. Can you hang on for another little while? I think they need to go out. What do you think?" I asked Barrett.

Barrett handed me the little ladies from his lap.

"I don't think that's a good idea," he said giving me an intense look. "If you don't want to get stuck here, we need to be quick. I'm pretty sure you want to be on your way."

I nodded.

"Okay. I'll do a quick check, gas up and we'll be off."

He shut the plane's door and jogged off in the direction of the building, quickly disappearing into the veil of falling snow. I looked around. I couldn't see much of the property through the denseness of the trees. The forest would no doubt be lush in the summer and glorious in the fall. Now, it had a decidedly Christmassy feel with snow settling on pine and spruce boughs, I also envisioned the shadowy forest in Hansel and Gretel. I shivered when chills crawled along my spine. I shook my head.

Stop being so dramatic.

A few of the dogs tried pushing forward into the cockpit and I had to keep them back. I heard scratching behind me. One of the dogs was pawing at the door and whimpering.

"Don't tell me. You have to pee, right?" I turned around and pushed the dogs on my lap off.

The dog scratching at the door turned his big brown eyes on me. If he could speak, I was sure he'd say *like a racehorse!* I glanced around, Barrett, was nowhere to be seen.

I checked my watch. He'd been gone only a few minutes and the dogs were getting restless. Did I dare I let the one dog out to go to the bathroom?

Decision made, I pushed my way to the back. I clicked the leash on to the retriever. That must be a universal sound that means "walkie" and the dogs set up another barking chorus

Continuous howls and barks echoed inside the plane. My ears rang. I had to settle the dogs somehow or my ears were going to explode.

"Okay, dogs, everybody calm down." They refused to listen. I maneuvered myself to the door, knowing I had to plan this properly. Be swift and precise. I didn't need any escapes and the vision of a swarm of dogs spilling out of the plane and vanishing into the forest could not become a reality.

But we had more flying ahead and if some were that desperate to go to the bathroom, it had to be now.

If I took them out individually, that might work. I opened the door a little and as I was shimmying out, with the retriever pushing me and the weight of the other dogs behind me, I knew they all wanted out so it was going to be difficult.

"Back, back off, everybody." I slipped out and breathed a sigh of relief. "Chalk up one for me. No great escape."

Opening the door a crack, I reached inside, took the retriever's leash. Now came the tricky part. Getting him out without releasing the rest.

"I hope this works." I took a breath and opened the door a little wider. "Okay, you. Out you come."

The dog pushed his nose at the crack of the door – then the two dogs behind him, both big and powerful, crowded the retriever. He jumped out, flinging the door wide, knocking me down. Before I could get to my feet, a waterfall of dogs followed them off the plane. They ran around in the snow barking happily. Many were doing exactly what I knew they needed to do, relieve themselves.

I jumped up and yelled for them

"Dogs, dogs! Back here. Come. Treat-treats." I

slapped my leg and was glad that at least I had a leash on the retriever. The rest of them were excited to be loose. I tried to pick up the little ones as they ran around. I scooped up a couple but the rest scampered away. The Pyr knocked me down and I tumbled onto my back. I should have fallen earlier because lying in the snow was a total magnet for the dogs. A pile of them jumped on top of me, barking and licking my face. I lay there and I realized there was nothing I could do except try and hang on to their collars.

It was dogs on the loose instead of dogs on the plane.

I rolled over and scrambled to my feet, keeping hold of two, and the rest scattered. I let out a whimper, utterly deflated. I tied up the two and got a bag of treats from the plane. Shaking the bag, I tossed a handful on the snow. Bribery works every time. At least I hoped so.

I picked up the two little ones and put them back in the plane.

"Come on, dogs, dogs, treats! Come and get 'em." I rustled the package and heads popped up, ears alert.

I shook the bag again. "Come and get 'em." I took out another handful and tossed them closer to the plane. The pack came bounding, snow flying. The snow was piling up fast and getting deep.

How was I going to explain to Barrett that I'd done the exact opposite of what he'd asked?

I had a handful of leashes, I quickly snapped them to their collars and fed the handles through another longer leash, while I continued to toss treats at their feet. It seemed to be working and soon I had them all collected and leashed together. I breathed a sigh of relief, smiling at the bunch of tangled dogs. I was rather proud of myself if I did say so.

I hadn't thought it was possible for the snow to come down any more heavily. The runway was barely visible and the drifts were growing. I felt a sinking sensation. Would we be able to take off?

The dogs pulled on the leashes and I threw more treats. At this rate, the large bag would be empty in no time.

I counted the dogs.

Damn! I was missing three and needed to find them before Barrett got back.

Just then—of course—the door to the building banged open and he stepped out.

"What the heck happened?" He looked at the dogs. "How did they get off the plane?"

"Well..." I hesitated and wound the leash around my hands. "Um...they got out."

"I can see that." I heard the exasperation in his tone and while I felt guilty about this situation, I still felt it had been the right thing to do. Or to attempt, anyway.

"I'm sorry, a couple were scratching to get out and I thought giving them a quick chance to relieve themselves would be wise, since we still have some flying to do. When I opened the door, there was a rush...and then I waved my hand and frowned.

He nodded, his mouth set in a grim line. "Well, looks like you're missing some."

"Yeah." I shook the treat bag and frantically searched the trees, hoping to see them running toward us. "In there somewhere."

"Well, we're screwed now. We're getting damn close to being snowed in at the rate it's coming down."

My stomach turned over and I felt sick. What had I done?

"I've seen planes fly in snow before. Why can't we just leave after we find them?" I was rambling and trying to find a solution.

"I don't think we have enough time to refuel at the rate this snow is coming down and then we look for the dogs." He shook his head. "Rather than risk it, let's get these in the hangar, find the others and call it a day." I followed his gaze down the runway, now barely visible. "We won't be going anywhere in this storm."

He looked up at the sky. Thick, fat flakes landed

on him, and the color of his eyes popped in the weird light cast by the storm. His dark hair, beard and mustache were dotted with snow, his skin still tanned from the time he'd spent outdoors. The forest and tall trees did little to diminish his stature, which seemed just as big and majestic as the wilderness around us.

And his eyes. Those blue, blue eyes...

He belonged here. This was his world.

And I was stranded in it with him.

"Come on, let's get these dogs inside. I want to get the plane in here, as well." He opened the big folding doors of the cavernous building.

I did as he said and brought the dogs in. We closed the door once we'd got them settled inside the building.

"Right then, let's go out and find those dogs." He said and collected the other leashes and the treat bag I'd put on a shelf.

With the big doors closed, the building was a welcome shelter, even if it was cold. I couldn't imagine spending the night here, but it was better than being under a tree or in a snowbank.

Barrett flicked a switch by the main door. The forest lit up like a stadium and the spotlights on each corner of the building turned the darkening forest into daylight, chasing away the gloomy fairytale feeling.

The snow appeared to fall even more thickly and the lights cut into the forest like a knife. The snow sparkled in the light, and the trees grew heavier under the weight, creating arches of the bowed branches.

Despite its beauty, I shivered, imagining evil monsters lurking beyond the edge of the gloom.

I refused to allow negativity to take over and forced myself to remain positive that we'd find the dogs safe and sound.

I followed Barrett outside into the blizzard, staying close to him. The wind and snow whipped at us and I was instantly frozen, cursing myself yet again for my attire.

But I hadn't expected the blizzard of the century.

Or being stranded.

In the wilderness.

With eleven dogs and one very sexy man,

6

"The lights should help us find them. Dogs, dogs!" he yelled. His voice boomed through the trees "Come on, dogs! Let's go."

"Dogs, dogs! Treats. Treats!" I yelled and pulled my jacket tighter around me while trying to shake the treat bag.

Barrett didn't appear too pissed off. He was annoyed, and I didn't blame him. I was annoyed at myself.

Barking echoed through the trees. Followed by a howl.

"Shh." Barrett held up his hand.

"Was that a wolf?" I whispered.

"Wait here." He didn't have to tell me twice. I backed up to a tree and kept my eyes fixed on the darkened edges of the forest. When he returned, I took his arm, my fingers brushing against cold, hard steel.

"You have a gun?" I was shocked, surprised and strangely comforted knowing he had one. Not that I condoned shooting anything, except in self defense...

"You never know when you might need it out here." He carried it in the crook of his arm with the muzzle pointed down, and put his arm around my shoulders.

"R-really? I'm such a city girl," I muttered to myself.

"The wilderness isn't for everyone." His voice was soothing and his strength evident. I didn't want break the connection. As long as we were close like this, I was safe.

"Do you hunt?" I couldn't bear it if he said yes.

"No, the gun is only for protection. Come on." His arm dropped from me and he took my hand. I gripped his as if it were a lifeline.

We walked farther into the forest, the lights behind us not as bright. The snow was deeper and I had to let go of his hand. I didn't want to, but he was breaking up deep snow with his powerful stride and it was easier to follow in his footsteps. My feet were really starting to get cold. I glanced around the forest with a new fear. Bears, coyotes and wolves could be anywhere

"We'd better find those poor dogs before something else gets them," I said, still keeping my voice close to a whisper. "Plus, I'm freezing."

"My thoughts exactly. Shake that bag of yours again," he suggested and turned to me. "If we don't find them soon, we'll have to go back and get you warmed up."

I nodded and shook the bag. We simply couldn't leave any dogs out here alone. We both yelled into the gloom of night. A few minutes later, the two beagles found us, coming at us in a fury, yipping and barking, practically jumping into our arms. We each picked one up.

"I can't fit her inside my coat. Can you take both?" I was embarrassed I'd gone for style rather than warmth and function on this trip. Live and learn.

"Poor things are shivering." Barrett took the dog I handed him and zipped them both up in his jacket. "Yeah, you're probably just as cold as these guys. Don't worry, we'll get you warmed up once we're back."

I nodded; the thought of heat almost made me lightheaded. "Thanks. I hope the husky hasn't gone far." I worried about him. And even if I had to stay up all night calling and shaking the bag, I would. Of course, I'd be doing it from the safety of the hangar doorway.

"Well, at least he's a northern breed, so if he ends up staying out for the night he'll be okay." I couldn't tell if Barrett meant it or was appeasing me.

I was glad the spotlights on the building were still casting light this far into the bush; even if it wasn't as bright, it helped.

Twigs snapped and the sound of a body rushing through the bush reached us. Barrett pushed me behind him and lifted the rifle.

"What is it?" I whispered and placed my hand on his solid back.

"Hopefully it's just the dog." His voice was almost a whisper.

Seconds later a gray streak burst out from the dark through a snow-covered bush and raced toward us with a happy howl.

"Oh!" I let out a little yelp, relieved to see the escaped husky. I reached in the bag for some treats and he rushed up to us. Barrett clipped the leash onto his collar while the dog snuffled the treats out of my hand.

"Thank God," I said, petting his head. "I have to admit, though. He looks pretty darn happy after having a run like that."

"I'm sure he is. I don't expect they got much freedom in the shelter or their foster homes," he commented. "Come on. Let's get back and get you warmed up."

"Sounds like a plan. And, no, I expect they don't. I don't really know their history other than that they were in the shelter that caught fire and luckily they were all saved and fostered in the interim."

Finally, bathed in the bright lights from the building, I was eager to get inside. Barrett closed the door behind us.

"Okay, that's it. We're here at least for tonight and possibly tomorrow as well –

"Two nights!" I was deflated. "One is enough, but two?" I didn't want to say I'd only brought a bag with limited contents since I'd had no reason to expect I'd be stranded. Was I ashamed to even contemplate that being stranded in the wilderness with Barrett, was, um, rather exciting?

He looked at me and the intensity of his gaze didn't hold any accusation. He dwarfed the desk he was standing beside, and I swallowed, licking my cold, dry lips, thinking how nicely his could warm them up.

Warm *me* up. I felt a surge of desire so foreign and breathtaking it almost knocked me to my knees. How could I be thinking such things at a time like this?

But I was.

He was struggling with his zipper and the dogs

were squirming with their heads poking out under his chin. I walked over to him, my legs a bit shaky.

"Hey, are you okay?"

I wanted to lean in to him. Glad of his nearness, his strength, protection ... and sheer manliness.

"Yes, I-I'm okay. Just got a bit wobbly." *When I thought of you kissing me.* I rested my palms on his chest and felt the wriggling inside his coat. "Let's get these dogs out of your coat."

I reached over to pull down the zipper, the warmth of his neck heated my cold fingers and our gazes met. He smiled, his neatly trimmed dark beard and mustache dusted with snow.

We continued to stare at each other as he let me unzip his coat, revealing the two excited dogs next to his warm, and impressive, flannel clad chest. I unzipped most of the way down, then pushed the coat open, reaching for one of the dogs. I let my hands linger against the flannel, my eyes closing for a few seconds to steady my racing heart.

It would be easy to unbutton the shirt, and slide my hands inside. I was struck by the sheer eroticism of the moment. Raising my eyes, I was sure his reflected the same. I cleared my throat and bundled one of the dogs into my arms.

"Uh, I suppose, er, we should settle them." I was all trembly and struggled for coherent words. "A-are we really stuck here for two nights?"

Suddenly that prospect was a little more exciting.

He nodded. "It's likely. Chances are the runway will be drifted over, and this storm doesn't look like it plans to let up anytime soon."

We stood staring into each other's eyes again.

I nodded. "Well, okay then. We'll have to make the best of it." I looked around. "Is there a heater in here, blankets or anything we can use to make a nest for the dogs, and for us? You know, to stay warm."

"Body heat works well." He winked and I nearly died.

"Um yes, I suppose it does. And doggie heat, too."

He threw back his head and laughed, it was deep, and rumbled through me. Oh Lord, I was a goner.

"What's so funny?" I asked him.

"Nothing. *You're* funny. I can see you're worried and trying not to be, concerned about the dogs getting cold--and being stranded with me." He leaned closer and I held my breath. "Don't worry, I know that isn't high on your wish list, but here we are." He lowered his voice a little. "At least I can protect you and your dogs."

We fell into a silence that was electrified. Suddenly our dynamic had changed from pilot and passenger to… what? Man and woman. From protection to attraction. Temptation.

"Well, no, it's not that. I mean, well, not really. We're safe and that's what matters. Will I be able to let Tess know what's going on?" I didn't really want to tell my family, they would only use it as ammunition against me.

"Yes, you'll be able to let her know. Now, how about we get these dogs all settled? We may as well hunker down for the night, too."

I looked around the building again to see what we could use to make it comfortable.

"Now, don't let any of the dogs get loose." He gathered up all their leashes.

"Where are we going?" I took the leashes he handed to me.

He paused a beat. "Did you think we'd be staying in here?"

I nodded. "Well, yeah."

He smiled, and it was one more notch on the enchanted scale. "No, we won't be staying here. Follow me."

So I did, wrestling with the dogs and leading them to a door at the back of the building. Lights hung from the trees, illuminating our way. I was shocked by how much snow had fallen in the last few minutes. It was getting deep and was a slog to get through. We emerged into a small clearing by a lake where a log-and-stone cabin sat next to the water. Tall snowy pines ringed the building, and lights twinkled around the cabin, making the snow sparkle like diamonds. I was captivated.

"Oh, wow! It's beautiful. This is yours?"

"Yep, it's mine. Built with these two hands." He raised them up even with a fistful of leashes.

"You built this?" I was incredulous.

He nodded. "It's not big, but it's comfortable, and we'll be fine here until the weather lets up."

Under the overhang on the stone porch, we were shielded from the wind. The cabin was sturdy with its log-and-stone walls and a heavy wooden front door.

He unlocked it and pushed it open.

"After you." Barrett stepped aside and I ushered the dogs into a small vestibule with a glass-paned pine door. Through the shimmery glass, I could see inside. Barrett came in and closed the exterior door.

It was tight with all the dogs and we found ourselves trapped, our legs tangled in the leashes.

I staggered into him and he caught me in his arms. "Steady now." His voice, like hot honey, slipped around me in thick, warm waves.

Our eyes met and, yes, I had a feeling that something was happening between us. I liked it.

My mouth dried again, and I moistened my lips. "Thank you. That's twice they've done this to us."

"Anytime. And yes it is."

I knew if he kissed me, I'd welcome it. If he tightened his arms around me, I would respond. If he carried me off to bed, I would let him.

What happens in the wilderness stays in the wilderness.

7

I was impressed by how welcoming the cabin was inside. I'd expected something very rustic, a mountain-man cabin with the basics--raw wood, repurposed appliances, a well pump for water and a wooden framed bed with canvas straps for a mattress.

"Okay." Barrett leaned over to unclip the dogs he had on leashes. "Let them explore."

"I guess, if you're sure." I unclipped mine and immediately the dogs raced around the room inspecting their new digs.

I walked over to Barrett and stood beside him, close enough to feel his warmth, which made me want to lean in to him. I crossed my arms and smiled, the dogs inspected every inch of the cabin.

He shut the glass-paned door behind us and didn't say anything as we watched the dogs.

The cabin was full of sounds – clicking toenails on the hardwood floors, panting and snuffling as the dogs exhausted their curiosity in every nook and cranny.

"There are pails in the laundry and we can set up a water station for the dogs." I followed Barrett and was even more surprised to see a very neat laundry room, with an exterior door.

"A laundry room?" I asked and didn't try to hide my smile.

"How else do you expect me to wash my clothes? Pound them with a stick against rocks in the lake?" He chuckled and I snorted, trying to bite back a laugh. He has a sense of humor.

"I must admit, I wasn't expecting such a beautifully appointed cabin." I looked at him. "You're just one surprise after another."

"I like to keep people on their toes." He filled the buckets and placed them on a boot tray.

I was hoping he'd give me a little more insight into his wonderful hideaway in the woods. How had he learned those skills? Did he have any help building it? What had inspired him to build it?

"Dogs! Come here, dogs. Come and have a drinkie. Water, water." I clapped my hands to get their attention. The golden came over and dove his nose into the bucket. He drank and drank and when he lifted his head, it was as if he brought all the water with him. It streamed across the floor.

"Oh, wow, you're a messy one." I stood back to keep my chilled feet dry and looked around for a something to wipe up with.

"Towels in the cupboard." Barrett said from the doorway.

I got the floor covered in towels just as a few others trotted over, immediately followed by the rest. I shimmied my way out of the laundry room and watched them gather around their watering station. I was impressed they all waited patiently for their turn to have a drink.

Barrett was in the kitchen again, opening a cabinet that had all kinds of switches. He flipped them on and the front of the cabin was flooded with light.

"Oh, wow. This is incredible." I stood by the tall windows that overlooked the lake, curling my cold toes. Snow shrouded the scenery beyond the shoreline, which wasn't far from the cabin's deck. I didn't think I'd ever seen anything more beautiful. Gone was the dread and worry about the snow from earlier that day, replaced with awe, beauty and a sense of peace and tranquility that almost brought tears to my eyes.

I felt Barrett behind me.

"Gorgeous, isn't it?" His voice was low, warm.

I gave a delicate shiver and looked back at him. "Yes, I've never seen anything so wonderful."

I almost leaned back into him until a bunch of dogs jostled us and we stepped apart. I was left with a longing I hadn't felt...ever. And it was for this man. I was sure I saw something in his eyes, as well.

I was way out of my element here, yet being with Barrett and the dogs in the middle of a snowstorm and stranded for who knew how many days, I felt strangely content. Safe. Barrett was a protector, just as he'd promised. Nothing bad would happen to me or the dogs with him around.

Maybe something deliciously good would happen.

"I'm going out to get some wood, then we can start a fire. While I do that, explore the place, make yourself at home. You might want to put on something warmer, too. Everything should be up and running, and there's loads of food. Pantry is off the laundry room, with chest freezers full of meat, veg, breads, sweets if you have a sweet tooth. There's also dry-goods shelves in there."

"Okay, thanks."

He walked to the glass door, lifted a huge parka hanging on a hook, along with an array of additional outer wear. He put it all on, then grabbed the rifle that was on the shelf above the hooks. "I'll be right back."

He opened the door and left, leaving a flurry of

snow in his wake. My hands were cold and I shoved them in my jeans pockets. Yes, I needed to find something warmer, and a hot bath would be perfect just about now

I was glad to see the dogs had started to settle down, some lying on the floor and others still exploring.

Even though it was warmer in here than outside, more heat was definitely needed. The low overhang of the roof kept snow from piling up under the windows. A stairway climbed the far wall from the kitchen, leading up to what appeared to be a loft. Perhaps a bedroom? The wide plank stairs were as solid as the logs of the house. I opened another door under the stairs to find a small office. Once I'd switched on a few lights, the rooms became even cozier.

A wonderful stone fireplace sat between the tall windows that overlooked the lake. The mantel was a slab of live edge wood and the chimney rose to the ceiling, also an intricate weave of stone. The ceiling was vaulted and fans were slowing turning at its peak to distribute the warmth.

I was very impressed and wondered if Barrett had designed as well as built it.

I was sure the furniture, solid, rustic and exquisite, was also built with loving hands. Maybe even Barrett's hands.

.   .   .

THE DOOR BANGED OPEN, making me and the dogs jump.

Barrett dropped an armload of firewood into a large box under the coat hooks on the wall. He stomped the snow off his boots and shrugged out of his coat, replacing both in the outer entryway, then closed the door. I could see why it had been built into the cabin. To keep the snow, wind and cold out of the interior.

"Looks like the dogs have settled in," he commented. He arranged a pile of wood in his arms and walked over to the hearth, setting the logs on the grate.

"I'm really sorry to put you out like this." I clasped my hands together.

"Hey." He stood up, reaching for a long match in a brass container on the mantel. "I've learned to roll with the punches, and I'm glad we landed. Rather be on the ground than up there bouncing around, especially with all the dogs."

"Me, too." I watched him build the fire.

He had a calmness about him that eased my jangled nerves. As I watched him, his confidence comforted me.

He was a big man. Tall and solidly muscled. There was an inherent gentleness about him, too. I saw it in how he handled the dogs and used himself to shield me when we were in the forest; it blended exquisitely with his natural sexiness. The effect was a swoon-worthy fusion that I found intoxicating.

I didn't realize I'd been holding my breath until I had to suck in oxygen, which I did as quietly as I could.

Soon he had a fire crackling in the grate behind the iron screen.

The deep sofa swallowed me and I pulled a cedar-scented quilt over myself. I was chilled. Heat from the fire fanned out and the colorful quilt was heaven. I relished the thawing out of my limbs.

Barrett sat down at the end of the sofa with a sigh. The dogs gathered at his feet and a few jumped up on the couch.

"Do you mind if they do that?" I leaned forward, about to usher them down.

He shook his head. "Let them get comfortable. God knows if they've ever felt like this before."

And that endeared me to him even more.

We sat in silence and watched the fire. The clicking of nails on the plank flooring was the only sound, aside from the flames licking at the logs.

"This is nice." I rested my head back on the cushion.

He didn't say anything. I'd become used to his lack of conversation; he didn't waste words on small talk. It was refreshing not to have to constantly make inane conversation, something that was commonplace in my other world. The world of my family. Oh, I could adjust to this.

I must have dozed because a deep woof from the shepherd jolted me upright.

"Everything's okay," Barrett reassured me, obviously noticing my look of confusion.

It took me a moment to regain my bearings. "Mmm, I guess I nodded off."

"You did." He was still sitting on the sofa, the two mini-dogs who'd found solace with him on the plane snuggled into his lap.

I pushed the quilt off and was relieved that the room was now quite warm.

"I'm hungry. The dogs must be, too. And the dogs. I brought food for them, but it's still on the plane." I stood and stretched, feeling his gaze, which warmed me up even more.

"I can make us something." He shifted to move the dogs and I stopped him.

"No, stay put. I'll throw something together. Keep those girls warm and cozy." I rose and pushed the quilt toward him and was pleased when he pulled it over the sleeping pups.

"Thanks." He laid his head back on the leather and closed his eyes.

"This is a lovely place. Do you live here year-round?" I asked, opening the freezer to see what I could whip up. I knew how to cook, and for the briefest time, wanted to be a chef until my parents put a quick halt to that idea.

"It's home and I'm here as much as possible." He sounded tired.

I grabbed a loaf of French bread and a container of frozen butter, a box of chicken nuggets and frozen vegetables. While definitely not gourmet, it was good enough to fill the belly and take the edge off.

I put everything on the counter and opened various cupboards to look for spices. "Does it get lonely out here?"

He didn't answer and I glanced at him. Had he fallen asleep?

"No, it doesn't. I prefer it to the clamor of the city." He wasn't asleep.

"Ah, a lone wolf," I said softly. I put the butter in the microwave with a generous helping of garlic powder, then turned the oven on to preheat.

I worked in the kitchen, and liked it when Barrett joined me.

"No, not a lone wolf. I like the peace of nature and life without complications."

I couldn't tell if he was referring to me, and how our situation had suddenly become complicated.

"I didn't mean to—

He waved his hand and took a roll of parchment

paper from the drawer. "I'm prepared for the unexpected. Nothing's your fault." He lined the baking sheet and I placed a bunch of nuggets on it.

I was curious as to what kind of complications he meant, the complications he tried to avoid. I was a job. A paying job, and like he said, you had to be prepared for the unexpected. Our current situation, being stuck up here in his cabin, certainly wasn't anything I'd planned for, either.

"Oh, I forgot to phone Tess," I said and paused, holding a bowl and knife.

"Did you want to do it now? I can man the fort here. But there may not be service right now."

I shook my head. "It can wait. Do you have to file a flight plan or anything?"

He nodded. "Yes, and I advised that we were delayed and likely not to arrive today."

"Okay, good. At least Tess will have that info."

We fell into an easy silence. Pretty soon we had a platter of cheesy garlic bread, chicken nuggets and vegetables tossed in garlicky sauce, plus he'd managed to dig up a bottle of wine. We carried our food to the table in front of the fire and settled down on the sofa.

Shimmying between the sleeping ladies and the golden curled up in the opposite corner, we were side by side.

Heat from where our thighs touched flared

through me. Sitting beside him seemed suddenly intimate. I leaned forward just as he reached for a plate and his arm brushed my breast.

A jolt raced through me. Our eyes locked and we froze. I wanted to hang on to what was happening between us and held my breath.

Barrett smiled and handed me the plate, his eyes never leaving mine.

I took it and breathed, "Thank you."

"You're welcome."

A log snapped in the fire, sending a spray of sparks up the chimney. Snapping us back to present. But I liked that the way we'd settled into the sofa, side by side, touching in a wonderfully easy silence that I hoped held a promise of more to come.

8

———————

Barrett looked at Rebecca and at the canine faces staring back at him. While he was prepared for most things, as he'd told her, this stop in the itinerary was somewhat unexpected. Weather conditions had gotten worse very quickly...

He'd been unsure of this job from the beginning, not sure about having a pack of dogs in the plane. He was astonished by how quickly he'd warmed up to the dogs. Especially the two "little ladies" as Beca called them.

It was an unexpected and rather incredible experience. The dogs for sure, but Beca – she'd said he could call her that, since her friends did – was the even bigger shocker. This was such unfamiliar territory for her, he'd been sure their adventure was going to be a disaster. She'd handled it well so far.

Aside from the dogs escaping when she let them out to relieve themselves.

She was leaning back against the sofa. The golden had shifted and his head was now in her lap. She was gently twirling his ears; his eyes were closed, and he was snoring gently in what must be dog ecstasy.

The rest of the dogs had found places to settle, all facing them on the couch.

"Do you feel guilty?" he asked Beca.

She turned to him and raised her eyebrows." Mmm?"

"The gallery watching us. Look at that big one over there. The stream of drool from that dog's almost reaching the ground."

Rebecca's watched the big, white dog with gray-tinged ears and she smiled. "Oh, you mean how they keep a keen eye on us as we eat in front of them? Yes, and that reminds me. I have to get the food out of the plane."

He thought for a beat and reached for another bite of food. All heads lifted when he popped a chicken nugget into his mouth.

"Okay, yeah, I think we need to get that food. I feel guilty as hell eating when they're all staring at me."

"I can go," she offered.

"No, I will." He rose and looked down at her. Her

chestnut curls, wild around her shoulders, gleamed in the firelight. Even her eyes held a translucence in this lighting. His chest tightened. He was responsible for her safety and perhaps he'd been a bit cavalier trying to stay ahead of the storm. "Uh, I think I might've pushed it with that storm on our heels."

He was shocked as hell he'd said it out loud. He'd just opened himself up to possible legal issues if something went wrong. Damn.

"*What*? You deliberately flew when we shouldn't have?" She was angry and he let her rant. "I'm not sure if I should be pissed off at you or just glad that you landed us here." She was sitting tall on the sofa and downed the last of her wine.

"I'm sorry for misleading you. But things changed faster than I expected..." He walked to the fireplace and removed the screen. Sparks flew up the chimney and hungry flames leapt to life when he shoved at the logs with the cast-iron poker. She didn't say anything further and he hoped she'd chill about it, otherwise it would make for a very difficult few days together. "I'll head out for the food now."

She stared out the window. "Will you be able to find your way?"

He smiled. *She's definitely not a country girl.* "It's not far."

"But you said there are wolves and bears and it's snowing so hard."

"Yes, but I'm comfortable in the wilderness, and I respect it." He rounded the sofa to the front door. "Worried about me?"

She jumped to her feet and the dogs followed her lead, then raced over to crowd around his legs as he pulled on his parka and shoved his feet into his boots.

"Worried? Hardly."

He bit back a smile, seeing how she turned away and crossed her arms. Yup, she was worried.

"I'll take the shepherd with me. You stay here. Lock the door behind me."

"You'll be all right? Nothing will happen to you?" The alarm in her voice was a sharp reminder that not everyone was comfortable in the wilderness. He knew lived in the city and he had to remember that.

"There's no reason to worry." He walked over to her and reached for her hands. She'd been wringing them together again and he took them in his. It pained him to feel the way she trembled. "Really, don't be afraid."

She studied him, as if assessing his words and trying to decide whether to believe him or not. A variety of emotions played across her face, and he wanted to drag her next to him and wrap her in his arms to prove she had nothing to be frightened of. This emotion was like being struck by a 2x4. He'd never felt this intense urge to protect someone before.

"You weren't truthful about flying in this weather and that makes it hard to believe you now."

"Fair enough. I'm sorry, I should've let you know about the weather as soon as I found out—although the forecast did change. But trust me now when I tell you there's nothing to worry about."

She chewed her lip and then nodded. "I'm not keen on you going out into the dark and blizzard. What if you get lost out there."

Barrett laughed. "I won't get lost. Now, where is this guy's leash?"

He was still holding her hands and her fingers curled around his. Gently he disentangled them, which left his hands feeling unbearably empty.

Beca took one of the leashes hanging over the hooks and clipped it onto the dog's collar, handing him the end.

He looked down at her and a sharp pain in his chest startled him. Her wide eyes, rimmed in thick lashes, the flush on her cheeks and her pursed lips filled him with a yearning that was almost painful.

It was an emotion he'd never felt before, and it shocked the hell out of him that he wanted more of it.

He put his hand on her shoulder, wanting to ease

her worry. "Honestly," he said in a gentle voice. "I promise you, everything will be fine. I'll be right back. I'll knock three times on the door so you know it's me."

Rebecca nodded and he picked up his rifle. He stepped outside, the shepherd following. Barrett waited until he heard the lock bolt behind him before heading off down the path.

He hadn't turned off the exterior lights and the path was well-lit under the heavy curtain of snow. The dog walked right at his heels without pulling with ears alert and nose busy sniffing all the scents that must be new to her...him? He checked.

She was a her.

He'd also strung a lifeline through the trees to the hangar, in case the power went out. In this blizzard, he was thankful for it, and the lights. Visibility was minimal and even though he knew these woods, it was easy to get lost in them, especially during a snowstorm. Getting disoriented and walking in circles, eventually losing the way and freezing to death was not the way he planned to leave this world.

The dog sniffed the snow and paused, looking up at him. He stopped and she relieved herself. He was patient and lifted his face to the onslaught of snow. He loved nature. It did his soul good to be out here in the wilderness. Patience was a hard-earned and welcome trait, one he'd learned over the years as he'd adjusted to how his life had gone.

The dog finished her business and pulled on the lead as if to say, "'let's get cracking." He drew in a deep breath. Yes, the wilderness was his world and he had to make sure that nothing happened to Beca or her dogs while they were here.

The shepherd fell into step beside him and they pushed their way through the drifting snow. Inside the hangar, he unclipped the dog. She immediately did a perimeter check and sniff-tested everything she walked past before returning to stand beside him by the plane.

"Hey, girl. Did your investigation? All clear?" He scratched her ears and she looked up at him with her deep brown eyes. For some crazy reason, it choked him up. "Now, how did you manage to make me feel like that? Must be those gorgeous eyes of yours."

She pranced on her two front feet, wagged her tail and then sat, still watching him, her tail swishing back and forth.

He was moved. "What got you into this situation, huh, girl? You seem trained and very well-behaved." He sucked in a breath. He was struck by the sudden reality that all of these dogs were homeless for one reason or another, and he couldn't even imagine the abuse and neglect some of them must have suffered.

He looked over his shoulder. The shepherd still sat, watching him intently while he got out the bag of food.

She was like a sentinel.

Barrett grabbed the small knapsack behind the two large bags of food. Beca might need some of whatever she'd packed inside.

At the door, he clipped on the leash while she sat patiently, ears alert and watching him with her intelligent eyes.

"You're a good girl, aren't you?"

The dog tilted her head to one side. Barrett laughed under her inspection. She was a beautiful dog. What kind of person would abandon a dog like this? Or any dog, for that matter.

He'd long ago shaken his hesitancy around dogs after being attacked when he was a kid. But he was still wary and accepting this job had taken a lot of consideration. When he'd seen the dogs barreling down at him on the tarmac, he'd found himself tightening up with anxiety. But once they'd been loaded on the plane, his caution had subsided and then, when flying, the way they'd crawled all over him and Beca had shed any lingering hesitation.

"Well, Missy, are you ready to head back out into the snow?" She wagged her tail and stepped toward the door.

He slung the knapsack over his shoulder, then

hefted the bag of food under his arm and balanced the rifle in the crook of his other arm. The last thing he'd ever expected was to be walking through the bush to his cabin, where a woman and a pack of dogs were waiting for him, while he led another one in the middle of a snowstorm.

A snowstorm he was pretty sure wasn't going to let up anytime soon, which meant they'd be here a couple of days, minimum. He found himself smiling at the prospect of being cooped up with Beca and the dogs.

They trudged through the snow drifts, and his sense of anticipation made him feel a bit jittery. The dog beside him did an excited hop and looked at him with interest.

"What? You feel it too? Like almost anything could happen?" Barrett hadn't met anyone like Rebecca before, and he was intrigued. Perhaps too intrigued for his own good. And hers. Their lives were so vastly different, without any common purpose. So, if something was going to happen between them, it would be a momentary fling.

9

———————

I watched Barrett charge off through the snow and trees with the dog and his rifle on his way to the hangar.

I took the opportunity to familiarize myself without being too nosy. Some of the dogs followed me upstairs, doing their own bit of recon. The cozy loft bedroom had a black iron railing. The bedroom overlooked the living area below. Windows rose to the vaulted ceiling, and I'd bet the view was incredible, although right now, I couldn't see much of anything through the blizzard. I was pleased to see a fireplace in the corner, which gave the room a very romantic allure.

I stood by the window and looked out into the dark and snowy night. The bedroom was reflected in the glass and I turned around.

There was a king-size bed in the center of the room by the iron railing. It was a far cry from the slatted bed I'd imagined. I walked over to it and fingered the chunky cable knit throw tossed over the footboard. Its softness tempted me to pull it around my shoulders, I left it on the bed and ran my fingers over the coverlet rather surprised the bedding was high quality.

It wasn't hard to let my imagination run wild and images of us between the sheets filled my mind.

Bedside tables held rope-wrapped table lamps with burlap shades. The room was tastefully decorated and cozy. Was he really this creative? I hesitated at the top of the stairs to have a last look at the bedroom, then descended, dogs hot on my heels.

The deck at the back – or front of the cabin, it was hard to decide which – faced the lake. I cupped my hands around my eyes and leaned closer to the glass.

Tarps tied around what I thought might be patio furniture flapped in the wind. I saw a hot tub in the corner.

Oh, that would be lovely. Sitting in the bubbling hot water with a glass of wine, the snow falling. Perfection.

It was shocking, really, how the day spent saving the dogs, and especially the flight, had gone through such a dramatic change. While landing here wasn't ideal, it was practical; There were things I hadn't anticipated, which of course I'd be prepared for the next time. I was grateful for Barrett's knowledge. Otherwise, this could have turned out to be a complete disaster.

I sighed, feeling content, and decided to clear the table. I wasn't sure if Barrett would want anything more to eat, but I knew it would be far too tempting for the dogs to leave it within sniff and lick distance.

They watched my every move. I put all the dishes in the kitchen and the food we hadn't eaten yet into the refrigerator for later.

A loud bang at the door set all the dogs into a barking frenzy, and I nearly jumped out of my skin. The logical part of me knew it was Barrett; the other part imagined Sasquatch clamoring to get in.

The dogs raced to the doorway. I wove my way through them, unlocked the door and snow blew in with Barrett and the shepherd. The dogs all set up a commotion and rushed around his legs.

"Well, this is quite a greeting," he said as he kicked off his boots, put them on a rack, placed the gun on the shelf and shook the snow off his parka. "Looks like you brought in as much snow as there is outside." I laughed and took his parka to hang up. The shepherd leapt over the smaller dogs and immediately went for a drink, followed by the others. I imagined them having a conversation about everything that had happened out in the snow.

Barrett closed the glass door to the vestibule and went into the kitchen, setting the bag of food on the butcher-block island.

"It's a good thing you brought food," he said as he ran his hand through his hair, which made it sexily messy.

"I hope the two bags will last us." I looked for bowls, collected almost a dozen and put them on the island.

"Yeah, me too." He paused. "Don't be too disappointed, but I think this storm is settling in for a while. It's getting worse out there." He opened the bag and began to scoop food into the bowls. The dogs rushed over and swarmed around us. We were the center of attention, all eyes trained on us.

"Do you think so?" I asked and picked up a few bowls for the little dogs. "Tess is going to be worried. We're expected and they'll think the worst." Even though my parents strongly disapproved of this venture, I knew they would still worry.

"I know you're concerned. We'll try for cell service again. Remember, I did radio in the change before we landed."

I nodded. "Yes, that's right. But it would make me feel better to speak with Tess myself, at least confirm that the message was passed on. You did say we'd have contact?"

I stood and took another dish from him, watching him fill more bowls.

I didn't know him at all. Sure, we'd talked before, when we'd first connected and while we made our arrangements, which definitely helped. He held a mysterious aura, a calm that comforted me, and yet he seemed a bit evasive. I felt a crazy jumble of emotions, especially now that we were stranded in the middle of nowhere.

I picked up another couple of bowls and moved away from him, a hot prickle of alarm racing down my spine. My mind was running away with me, and that had to stop.

"Yes, I know I did." He took the last of the bowls and we stood there staring at each other. His expression was the same as always, and I didn't see any kind of insidious intent in his eyes.

Did he know my background? My family? The wealth? *What if he's going to kidnap me for ransom? Or...worse. Damn my overactive imagination! Calm down, Beca!*

My gaze ran over the dogs busy watching us, tails wagging, tongues out, and then back to Barrett.

"What's wrong?" he asked, brows furrowed.

I shook my head and looked away. "Nothing. I'll take these bowls into the pantry."

I put them down and sorted out the smaller dogs who'd eat in here. Then I drew in a deep breath and listened to him talking to the other dogs.

"Come on, guys. Chow time. You, big boy, stay here with this bowl. Hey! No, come on over here. This is your bowl." He chuckled.

I smiled and gave myself a shake. I was being stupid about this. I closed the door to the pantry and peered around the doorjamb. He was surprisingly patient as they followed him around the kitchen, waiting for him to set the bowls down. He was like the Pied Piper, except with dogs.

This man wasn't dangerous. Nah, no way.

BARRETT PUT the last of the bowls down for the dogs. He was glad they all seemed to be settling in quite well. But he wondered what was wrong with Beca. Her mood had taken a turn and he wasn't sure why.

He replayed their conversation and didn't think anything they'd talked about was a concern. She'd settled down, just like the dogs, but something had changed and he couldn't figure out what.

He understood her worries about being here with him.

Stranded with a stranger.

He knew he was a good guy. But they were strangers to each other, and he thought about the situation from her point of view, acknowledging that she'd put her life in his hands. He watched her fuss about in the kitchen. Her movements were slow and she pushed her hair out of her eyes, then pressed her fingers to her forehead.

He could tell that she felt powerless. Felt a loss of control. He understood that and had to make her feel more comfortable. He'd have to do a better job of it.

They'd talked quite a few times, via phone and live video, before finalizing this rescue flight. At least they had that. He'd been intrigued by her and her project. Which was why he'd agreed to fly the dogs. He wanted to learn more about her.

Maybe if he just talked and filled the silence in the cabin, it would make her feel more relaxed.

"You want to watch something?"

She looked at him. Damned if his chest didn't tighten. He could see she was still upset and the last thing he wanted was for her to feel uncomfortable because of him.

"Do you have cable?" she asked, giving the counter a last swipe with a cloth.

"No, but I do have satellite. Or DVDs, even some

old VHS tapes." He smiled and was rewarded with a smile in return.

"How can you have satellite reception if you have no phone reception?"

Ah! that's what it is. She hasn't contacted her people.

He should've known. He had to remember she wasn't used to being in a situation like this, unlike him.

"You're right. I'm sorry. Hopefully tomorrow we'll be back on line," he offered.

"I hope so!" Beca pulled her phone out of her purse. "I checked earlier and there was no signal." She held up her cell, moving around the cabin. "Nothing, nada, zip."

"Let's see if we can get you logged into my Wi-Fi."

He led the way into the office and sat behind his big wooden desk. He gave her the information.

"It's not working. Do I have it right?"

He glanced at her phone. "Yep. Give me a sec."

Barrett checked the Wi-Fi settings and then the modem. "Okay, we have no connection, which means we don't have satellite. Unfortunately, we can't send emails or texts."

"Oh, my God! See, landlines would work at times like this." She paced around his office; Barrett felt energy pour off her and knew he'd have to calm her down.

"Look, let's try a radio call."

"Okay, great!" She came over to stand beside him to look at the computer screen.

She was so close to him that he felt the heat of her body, and her delicate scent reached his nose. He cleared his throat and pushed the chair back.

"Not the computer. A radio.

I PUT the mic back down on the table after speaking to the forest station, who said they'd get a message to Tess. I let out a deep sigh. Relief.

I felt ashamed that I'd suspected him of not being honest.

"Thank you. Now I can calm down." I flopped onto the couch and immediately a couple of the dogs jumped on top of me, licking my face. I laughed, enjoying their attention. Through the jumble of dogs, wet tongues and hair in my face, I watched Barrett standing by the fire. He was smiling at me.

"I'm glad that worked out with the radio," he said. "Sorry I didn't think of it sooner."

I gently pushed the dogs away and several of them curled up beside me on the couch. "It's okay. My mind ran away with me and I overreacted a bit." I didn't want to tell him I'd become suspicious.

"It's all sorted now. Tomorrow I'll check the

satellite dish, make sure it isn't covered in snow." He paused. "How do you feel about going in the hot tub?" He raised his eyebrows and smiled.

"Ah, um..." My heart leapt in my chest at the thought of immersing myself in the hot water, with him. "I've never been in hot tub in the middle of a blizzard."

He laughed, the sound deep and powerful.

"You're in for a treat, then. There's nothing like it."

"What can I wear? I didn't bring a bathing suit." I raised my shoulders. "The last thing I ever expected was hot-tubbing in the middle of the wilderness with a pack of dogs and in a snow storm no less!" I started to laugh.

"I hope you're not referring to me as a dog." He smiled again. "More wine?"

"Sure. Thanks."

"Wine and hot tubs go great together. And I have some shorts and a T-shirt you can put on, although they'll be way too big for you."

A thrill whispered through me at the thought of wearing his clothes. Otherwise it would be naked hot tub time. And if I was totally honest with myself, I wasn't opposed to the idea. I was surprised at how quickly my thoughts had moved from alarm to contentment, and I had to admit he'd be the most charming hot tub companion.

"Perfect."

"I'll get you some. Hang on." I watched him go up the stairs to the loft. A minute later, he was back down with a neatly folded shirt and shorts.

"Thank you." I took the clothes and went into the bathroom to change. With my own clothes stripped off, I debated whether to keep my bra and panties on; they were the only ones I'd brought. I took them off and folded them inside my clothes, then pulled on the shorts, which had a drawstring and the T-shirt, which hung down to my hips.

Going braless, clad only in thin fabric, made me feel erotically exposed. My nipples stiffened against the soft cotton. I took a towel from the linen closet in the bathroom and wrapped it around myself.

When I came out of the bathroom, I stopped dead in my tracks. He stood there, holding two glasses and the bottle of wine, in a bathing suit, bare-chested. Oh, he had an excellent body.

Seeing him shirtless and without pants touched me in all the right places and I felt myself light up like a sparkler.

"I think the dogs should stay in," he said. "It's not fenced and they all seem rather content."

I nodded. "Yes. That's a good idea. Before we go to bed for the evening..." I paused and my gaze flickered at him because that was another potentially awkward situation in front of us. "They'll need to go out for a bathroom break."

"Mmm. I do have some snow fencing in the shed. Give me a few minutes to see what I can rig up."

"You'd do that?" I walked over to stand before him and looked out the window. "You mean here?"

"Yes, it'll keep them contained, and we won't have to take them out on leashes. And the lights shine on to the deck so we'll be able to see them better."

"Thank you." I took the glasses and wine from him.

He quickly pulled on his coat and boots in the front vestibule. "I'll be right back. Lock the door behind you because I'm going to go around to the lakeside."

I did as he asked and then watched out the window. The dogs were also very curious about what was going on. It didn't take him long to string up a roll of orange fencing from one side of the deck around a few trees to the other side, creating the perfect enclosure for the dogs.

He worked swiftly and efficiently. He was doing this for me and for the dogs. His whole world had been turned just as upside down as mine.

A new emotion was aroused in me. He didn't

have to do all this. But he *was* doing it and I felt very grateful. I was beginning to see what a good, kind man he was.

And yet in a few days we'd be parting ways to go back to our own lives... That made me sad.

10

Barrett indicated that I should open the door.

"Is it okay to let the dogs out?" I was worried one of them might escape through the fence. The last thing I wanted to do was traipse around in the bush trying to round up lost dogs.

"Yes. Let's see how they react. I'll keep an eye on them if you want to bring the wine and glasses out."

I pushed the door wider and the dogs rushed outside. The raced around, jumping and barking, sniffing and doing a perimeter check.

They were instantly covered in snow and I smiled at the joy they exhibited. Wine fixings in hand, I walked carefully along the path Barrett had shoveled out toward the hot tub. The lid was up and steam was rolling out of the bubbling water, mixing with the falling snow. "Careful, the steps are the icy."

He took my elbow and I stood at the top of the steps. He took the bottle and wineglasses from me and I clutched his hand while I stepped over the edge and into the hot water. Sinking beneath the bubbles, I let out a big sigh of delight.

"Oh, this is wonderful." I rested my head against the back and through the veil of steam and snow, watched him strip off his clothes and kick his boots aside. He was like a god emerging from the mist.

"How do you like hot-tubbing in the snow so far?" he asked once he'd settled on the seat across from me.

"It's wonderful." I ducked down lower in the water to cover my shoulders. "We should've put hats on."

"Sometimes I do. I can always get some if you want."

I shook my head. "No, don't get out. You've already done so much. Let's just enjoy the moment. Now, how about that wine?"

He smiled and reached for the bottle. I took a glassful of a beautiful red and sipped.

"I do have to say," I admitted, "this is the last thing I expected to happen today."

"Same here. But I'm not complaining."

"Do you live here year-round

"This is my home base, yes."

"How do you get supplies? Is there a road that comes in? It seems very remote."

"It is remote. Just the way I like it." He smiled. "There's a logging road that comes in off the main highway and I have right-of-way access to the service road that runs along the power-line cut. Access to my place is off that. Most of the time I fly in, though. The service roads aren't maintained through the winter." He smiled and I watched him sip his wine.

"Somehow, that makes me feel a little less stranded, knowing there's a road out there."

"Yes, although it's not accessible right now."

My heart fell. "Oh, I thought maybe it was another way out."

"Normally it is. But in the winter it's too difficult maintain."

"You mean it's easier to keep the runway open?" That seemed an odd thing to me.

"Actually, it is. I use it more and I need it ready for jobs. Like yours." He set the glass down on the edge of the tub and leaned back with his arms stretched across the edge. The muscles of his chest flexed and I was mesmerized.

I swallowed. He didn't have to try to be sexy. He simply was. And suddenly I was okay with being stranded out here in the middle of nowhere.

The tensions of the day floated off into the bubbling heat of the water. I was almost mesmerized by the way the steam drifted from the tub, caught in the whirlwind of snow that came around the barrier at the side of the deck.

The wine mellowed me and my empty glass was soon full again. Barrett had moved a little closer to me in order to top up the wine and I didn't mind at all.

He stayed where he was and I turned to look at him. His face had softened and his eyes also seemed less tense. He should relax more often, I thought. I supposed I should, as well.

We gazed at each other. Quietly.

I think I knew all along, since we'd first talked — and yes, okay, flirted — over the phone and by video, that there was an attraction.

It was as if we'd been subtly teasing each other. I could see it now, not so much at the time. We'd unconsciously been laying the groundwork.

And here we were.

I sipped more wine, loving the way it heated my belly. I didn't look away from him and felt my lips part. His eyes lingered on my mouth and he lowered his head.

Thrills raced through me. He paused, finding my gaze again. He raised his eyebrows, and I knew he was asking for approval.

I didn't turn my head away, giving him a gentle smile. The closer he got, the more my eyelids drooped until his lips found mine. I moaned into him, electrified by his kiss.

It was soft as a butterfly wing and I was the one who took the step to deepen it. My hand moved up his chest as I turned to face him. He held my waist when I moved closer, the cold air chilling the fabric of the t-shirt on my back. I pressed even closer, and his arms held me tight. Desire like I'd never felt before flooded me. I crashed my mouth down on his and ran my fingers up his neck and into his hair, which was delightfully frozen in little peaks.

His tongue swept across my lips and I opened to him. Now he was the one in charge and I welcomed him

We kissed for what seemed like forever until my body began shaking. The jets had automatically turned off, the water was still, and I hadn't noticed. My nipples touched the fabric of his shirt, and his hands slipped under the back of my T-shirt when it floated around me on top of the water.

His touch was glorious.

Our kiss was heaven.

His hands gripped my bottom and my knees rested on the seat on either side of his hips. He pulled me to him and I drew in my breath. Every hard plane, and ridge of his muscular, powerful thighs slayed me.

We were two lost pieces of a puzzle that fit together and completed each other.

BECA WAS BREATHLESS, as was he, and when she snuggled beside him in the hot water, he put his arm around her, not wanting to let her go. She sipped from her glass of wine. Barrett gazed out into the snow, keeping an eye on the dogs. The silence of the forest was beautiful.

The dogs snuffled around, and their paws squeaked on the snow. He was at home here in the wild, even though he had all the conveniences of modern life in the cabin, most of which he rarely used. It was the wilderness that spoke to his soul.

He tilted his head and listened. One of his favorite sounds was the soft hush as snowflakes descended from the dark sky and settled to create a velvety blanket.

"I think this is one of the most magical nights of my life," Beca whispered.

She leaned her head into his shoulder, and a rush of adrenaline shivered through his body.

He finished his wine before answering her. "There are many nights like this in the woods. Wait until you see the stars on a clear night. Or the Northern Lights. Or a full moon that's so bright it glitters through the trees to cast shadows on the ground."

"I've never seen Northern Lights." She sounded wistful.

"Then you'll have to come back so you can see them." He squeezed her slightly. He wondered if she took it as involuntary or intentional. He smiled when she leaned into to his side.

"I'd like that."

"Then we'll make it a date." Had her really invited her back? He was shocked and yet pleased by how things had happened between them. It felt like he'd known her for a very long time, not just a few weeks and only meeting face to face this morning.

Barrett looked down at her upturned face and lowered his for a kiss.

He didn't elaborate on his invitation for her to come back. He wasn't one to plan too far into the future, knowing that things could take a sudden turn at any time. Things would play out as they were meant to.

"I think we should go in." He stood and held out his hand. "It's a bit too cold to keep the little dogs out."

"I agree. But we'll freeze out of the water."

"Not if you're quick. Just don't slip on the snow."

He stepped out of the tub and the dogs gathered around his legs. "I think they want in."

She stood and he was captivated. The wet T-shirt clung to her, outlining her breasts, and his eyes lingered on her stiffened nipples before he took her hand to help her out.

Beca let go of his hand and let out a squeal. "Cold on the toes."

He watched her hurry to the door, followed by the pack of dogs. He closed up the tub and followed her with the bottle and glasses.

The dogs rushed around her and pretty much carried her into the cabin. She laughed with delight and it was then that he realized just how silent his life had been. It took this woman from a completely different world and a crew of love-starved dogs for him to see the gaping hole. A heaviness settled over him. The momentary brightness of her laugh was a reminder of what would be missing when he flew her home with the dogs.

"Careful," she told him. "The floor's slippery. I skidded on the floor and if I hadn't caught myself I'd be sprawling out in front of you."

"That would be a sight."

She was shivering. The T-shirt and shorts were dripping, leaving puddles at her feet. "I don't want to mess up your floors. Where did I put that towel?"

"I'm not worried about the floors. You look

cold." He gave her a wink and she glanced down at her chest, the fabric not hiding the press of her nipples against the wet T-shirt.

She didn't cover herself and he took her hand.

"Come in here." He led her into the laundry room and pulled a towel down from the shelf.

He wasn't expecting Beca to pull off her shirt and stand proudly, naked, before him. His breath froze. She was so perfect and he couldn't draw his eyes away. It took all his resolve not to sweep her into his arms. Instead and he shook out the towel and held it up.

She stepped into it and leaned against his chest. He wrapped the towel around her shoulders, rubbing up and down her arms. The towel was big and came down almost to her knees. As she shimmied in his arms, the wet shorts went *splat* on the floor and he laughed when she flicked them into the sink with her toe.

"Well, now..." He looked into her eyes, seeing the banked passion in them. "I didn't expect this, a naked woman standing in my laundry room."

He grinned and she gave a little laugh that sounded slightly nervous.

"Not naked. In a towel. And neither did I." She smiled.

"Let's get you by the fire and warmed up. He took another towel, wrapped it around his waist and kicked off his bathing suit. She'd hung up her wet clothes and he did the same with his.

They hurried into the living room and flopped onto the couch in each other's arms. He pulled the quilt over them.

"Oh, this is better," she murmured. Her damp hair lay on his shoulder and her breath was warm on his chest.

Lights were low and the dogs were curled up, finally resting and sleeping. The fire was warm but slowly dying. It was a hypnotic moment, and they fell into a comfortable silence, lying in each other's arms.

"I should fix the fire," he said in a low voice.

"No, stay." She gripped his arm. "I think I could lie here like this forever," she told him, snuggling into his side when he put his arm around her.

"Okay." Contentment swept through him, along with a shocking pang of sadness.

He was getting a taste of what it could be like to share your life with someone. An idea he'd never really contemplated despite various brief relationships. Well, *flings*, was a more accurate term, he supposed. Only once had he opened his heart to someone, years ago, and her death had nearly broken him. His throat restricted and he tightened his hold on Beca. Continuing to stare into the flickering firelight, he processed this emotion that shook him to the core.

He sighed. Beca had fallen asleep and sighed. He held her close, looking down at her still-damp hair.

She had reached deep inside him to a place he'd protected all these years. And now the crack threatened to burst open.

The urge to allow the feelings to surface warred against maintaining his determination to remain emotionally distant. It challenged him to wonder if maybe it was a habit to keep himself detached.

He rose and carried her upstairs and placed her on the bed. Covering her, he stood for a moment and watched her sleep. He wanted nothing more than to crawl into bed with her, hold her, make love to her, but he wasn't going to do that.

He had stuff to think about, and taking the step from kissing in the hot tub to sex in bed was a leap they both had to be sure about. He was highly attracted to her and sensed she was to him, as well. But now wasn't the time.

He turned on a dim light on the far side of the room so she wouldn't be startled if she woke before dawn. With a last look at her sleeping peacefully, he went back downstairs to double-check the dogs.

Everyone was fine. Everything was locked up. The snow was still coming down and the forecast called for at least another thirty-six hours of continued snowfall.

Which meant they'd likely have to stay here for the duration. At least until he could get the runway cleared.

Businesswise, it wasn't an ideal situation for him, especially with the Wi-Fi down, which put a hold on quoting any further contracts. He had to admit, though, that a bad situation had turned into something surprisingly good. He fixed the fire, and stretched out on the couch. Moments later, the two old ladies jumped on him and nestled on his lap. The glow of the fire, and knowing that all was well with his charges, finally allowed him to drift off.

His last thought was of Beca upstairs and the feelings she'd aroused in him. The desire to open to her, allow her in, was strong, but he feared what that might bring into his life.

11

———————

I opened my eyes to darkness and held my breath. Where was I? I lay silently, breathing softly, and listened to the sounds around me.

It had been a long time since I was afraid of the dark. As a child I would panic. Waking to blackness, not a speck of light--it was what I'd imagined death was like.

That same feeling rose in me now. I didn't move, just clutched the covers under my chin, searching for a glimmer of light. My eyes adjusted, and a soft, luminous glow stained the window from a light in the corner of the room.

I blinked and rubbed my eyes, letting out a ragged breath. Now I knew where I was. In Barrett's bed in the loft. Was he lying next to me? I reached my arm across and felt nothing except the cool sheets. Where was he?

Was I glad or disappointed he wasn't beside me?

I didn't remember coming up the stairs to bed, so he must have carried me. I lifted the cover to find I was still wrapped in the towel and quilt from last night.

I pushed sheets back and swung my legs over the side of the bed. Chilly air whispered across my shoulders and I pulled the quilt tighter.

If he wasn't in bed with me, where was he? I padded to the top of the stairs and peered into the darkness. Embers from the fire cast a warm glow. I tiptoed down the stairs, hoping not to disturb any of the dogs. Most of them lifted their heads when they saw me. I stopped at the end of the sofa and saw Barrett stretched out, bare-chested, another quilt thrown over his legs, and the two little ladies curled up on his lap. I smiled, hugged myself and rested an elbow in a fold on the quilt, and chewed the end of my thumb. He was fast asleep and I allowed myself a moment to appreciate the vision of his face relaxed in sleep. I had the urge to kiss him awake.

But I didn't.

The fact that he'd carried me upstairs and then slept on the couch told me he was a gentleman. Last night had also told me he had a powerfully passionate side. I drew in a soft sigh, strangely content.

I needed a drink and walked quietly into the kitchen, thinking about everything that had happened since yesterday morning, leading to the dogs and me stranded in the middle of a blizzard. Wind moaned around the eaves of the cabin and must have been what woke me. It was only 4:30 in the morning. Way too early to get up.

I filled a glass with water and carried it over to the window. It was still snowing and looked heavier than it had last night. We wouldn't be going anywhere today. I glanced over my shoulder at Barrett. He had one arm flung above his head, and the other one curled protectively around the dogs sleeping on him.

I was tempted to go back up to bed, my eyes burned and I could barely keep them open. I was exhausted, and rather than climb the stairs, I decided to join Barrett on the sofa. First, the fire needed stoking, and I gave it a go. Trying to be as quiet as possible, I poked the dying embers and added a couple more pieces of wood.

There was room for me to settle at the opposite end from Barrett; the couch was lovely and deep and it swallowed me up. I pulled another quilt from the basket beside the couch and tucked it around both of us, pausing when he rolled onto his side, not wanting to wake him.

Carefully I stretched my legs out next to him

and rested my head on the pillow. A wonderful sense of calm and contentment relaxed me as I watched the flicker of firelight play across the ceiling, enjoying the feeling.

The cabin – its hush broken by the snap and crackle of the fire, the soft snoring of dogs and the wind kept at bay outside – seemed exactly the right place to be.

I relaxed, liking the feel of Barrett's legs next to me. A couple of dogs moved to a new sleeping space, one joining another on the leather armchair, and the golden retriever lying down on the floor beside me, his nose rooting for my hand to pet him. Which I did. The shepherd went into the laundry room to have a drink. She came back and sat, leaning against the couch at Barrett's head. I smiled when I saw his fingers move almost imperceptibly, stroking her.

I watched Barrett sleep until my eyes closed.

BARRETT WOKE. There was a body next to him. Confused for a moment, he quickly got his bearings when he looked down to see Beca fast asleep at the other end of the couch. He smiled, and liked that she felt comfortable enough to share the couch with him. He rose, careful not to wake her, and covered her with his blanket. Some of the dogs watched what he was doing, their eyes following him around the cabin. He went into the washroom, splashed water on his face and came out to make sure all the dogs' water bowls were full. He was glad he'd put up the fencing last night, which made it much easier to let the dogs out to do their business without needing to leash them all.

As he ushered them out the door, he realized he was definitely growing accustomed to having them around. This whole trip had been full of contradictory events and emotions. He watched the dogs through the window and saw that although it was almost dawn, the sky was still dark. Blowing snow whipped around the cabin, moaning in the eaves.

He knew they wouldn't be able to leave until tomorrow at the earliest, depending on the track of the storm. It would more likely be the day after tomorrow before they could even think about it. He turned around to watch her on the couch. It wasn't hard having her here; in fact, it was easier than he'd expected. She wasn't as complicated or needy as he'd thought she might be—far from it. He pressed his lips together, feeling a little guilty that he'd assumed she would be high maintenance.

He brewed coffee and had a little of the food from last night. A dog barked outside and he rushed over to let them in, hoping they didn't wake her. Her breath was deep and he looked at her face, as if to imprint it on his mind.

Barrett set his mug on the table and slid onto the couch, lifting Beca's head and her pillow to rest on his lap. She let out a sleepy moan and rolled over onto her side. The dogs had settled down and he sat back, resting his feet on the coffee table, and enjoyed the coffee.

Sitting here, feeling quiet, relaxed, content, was exactly where he wanted to be. She said something in her sleep, murmured a few words that he couldn't make out, and he wondered what she was dreaming about.

Probably their bumpy flight yesterday and landing with the dogs. Or maybe she was dreaming about their session in the hot tub. Something he'd enjoyed, too. Would they take it any further?

He didn't even know if she had a partner, a boyfriend or even a husband. She was a gorgeous woman, smart, intelligent and a challenge any man would be lucky to have as his "significant other."

He smiled, imagining what it would be like to be with her on an everyday basis. Yep, pretty sure she'd keep him on his toes. Being with her these few days revealed his solitary life in sharp relief.

But with the lifestyle Beca came from—what he knew about it, anyway – he couldn't see her interested in remote living. A night or two maybe, but anything longer? He wasn't optimistic.

He chuckled. Getting way ahead of himself.

He pulled the quilt up over her shoulders, and while he was tempted to kiss her awake, he let her sleep.

12

The smell of coffee drew me up through layers of sleep. It was exactly what I needed.

"Sorry I barged into your space." I said, pulling the quilt around me, realizing I was still clad only in the towel.

"No problem." He stood. "I was surprised to find you down here on the couch when I woke up."

"I was a bit confused when I woke and wondered where I was, and then where you were. So I came down to check on the dogs and there you were, fast asleep on the couch, surrounded by dogs. I couldn't resist, and it was warmer here. I figured I'd join you. I mean, it's not like we're complete strangers anymore." I smiled and tilted my head sideways.

His grin widened and I enjoyed the rush of heat his smile brought me.

"Now then, you either need some clothes, which I can dig up for you, or...."

My cheeks heated and I chastised myself. I wasn't a blushing virgin, for crying out.

"Or what?" I stood in front of him and had the strongest urge to fling off the blanket and the towel and jump on him. But I couldn't. Would I kick myself with regret when I was an old lady remembering this moment?

My indecision must've shown on my face because he walked over to me. Put his hands on my shoulder and looked into my eyes.

"Or..." his voice was low and gravelly. I held my breath, knowing what was coming next. "We could go back upstairs together." He nodded at the loft before continuing. "Or just stay here on the couch and share the blanket."

I started to tremble and raised my hands to grasp his elbows.

"Surprise me." I looked at him from under a fall of hair. I let out a little *oh* when he swept me into his arms and carried me up the stairs.

A chorus of clicking dog paws chased us to the loft.

"Looks we have a posse following us." Barrett put me down on the bed.

"Aww, I don't mind if you don't," I said and watched the pups roam around the loft, sniffing.

"As long as none of them has a video camera. We don't need a sex tape making the rounds." Barrett smiled down at me and I laughed.

He leaned over me, and I was acutely aware of my nakedness beneath the quilt. The dogs, the whistling of the wind, snow pellets battering the window--it all faded away.

Excitement flared through me and I held my breath. I closed my eyes for a second to gather the courage to do what I wanted to do, then opened them and threw off the quilt. I gasped at the smoldering expression on his face.

"Oh, Beca...

He knelt on the bed and pulled me to my knees, holding me in his arms. I pushed at his shorts, and he managed to kick them off. My hungry fingers swept over his firm, rounded buttocks and up his muscled back.

Oh, Lord.

We clung together, and his skin next to mine nearly had me mindless. My body hummed wherever we touched. When his lips found my collarbone and blazed a trail to the curve of my neck, I hung useless in his arms.

I turned my head, needing his mouth on mine, and we merged together. Our tongues found each other. We breathed each other in. Chest to chest, hips to hips, we fell back onto the sheets.

Never had I been as charged with desire as I was now. We rolled on the bed until I was above him, leaning over him, my hair falling around us.

Our breath ragged, I let my knees open and straddled his hips. His arousal, powerful and strong, intoxicated me. I'd never allowed myself to be so free and bold with a man.

Was it because of our situation, the fact that we were unlikely ever to see each other again? Was it about the excitement of stranger sex? Or was it simply that I felt sexy and confident with him?

Right now I didn't care and I let the thoughts go, totally immersing myself in sensation. In *feeling*.

"P-protection?" I breathed the words into his neck after he'd pulled me down.

"Mmm, drawer."

We jostled around to reach the drawer, and I giggled seeing all the dogs in the room, some lying asleep, others simply relaxed. The golden had his head resting on the edge of the bed watching us, and the shepherd was standing as if on guard, facing the stairs.

"What's so funny?" Barrett put the wrapper on the bedside table and knelt, hooking his hands under my knees, pulling me onto his thighs so I was sitting on them.

"Look, we have an audience."

He glanced around and grinned.

"Well, how about we give them a show," he murmured and pushed me back onto the pillows.

"Oh..."

I forgot about the dogs, the snow, totally lost in Barrett and what we were doing with each other.

We peeled away the emotional layers, opening ourselves to each other. We were wonderful together, exquisite, and deep tears threatened.

I clutched him, as we met and fused and found our place among the stars together. Spent and content, tangled in the jumbled sheets, we caught our breath.

"Ah," Barrett said.

"What?" I asked in a sleepy voice.

"Dogs are licking my feet."

"Is that all? They love you. You're their savior and hero." *And you just might be mine, as well.*

The golden jumped on the bed and nuzzled up to me, resting his head on my hip. The two little ladies also managed to scramble onto the bed and worked their way between us.

"What if they all try to climb up here with us?" I heard the humor in his tone.

"I sure hope your bed's strong." I shifted to see his face. He looked happy, as happy as I was feeling right now.

He moved in for a kiss and the little dogs between us gave a whine.

"I think you'll have to wait," I told him, "until the
ladies say it's allowed."

13

Bundled up in a spare parka, hat and gloves of Barrett's, I slipped my arm in his as we walked in the forest. The boots were too big for me, but way better than mine. Some of the dogs were off leash because they stayed close to us and, as usual, a few of the others had to be controlled.

The snow had let up a little bit, and there were patches of blue sky, but the drifts were deep as we wove between the trees. I was pooped almost right away. A sad state of affairs that told me I was way out of shape.

The forest seemed to have come alive. I heard woodpeckers and other birds, and the wind still attacked the tops of the trees, making the branches snap and crack like gunfire.

"Do you think it's going to snow again?" I asked, breathless.

"It might. Radar showed another front coming in. I guess it depends on which way the temperature goes. Either it'll turn to rain or sleet or back to snow again."

I glanced up at him. "Think we'll be stuck here another day?"

This smile ran off his face and he tightened his lips. "Would that be so bad?"

I sensed I'd hurt his feelings and thought about it for a moment. I wasn't sure how to answer. *Would it be bad?* I watched the dogs romping around the trees investigating their new freedom then looked at Barrett, about to answer, but hesitated when I saw his frown.

"Um, if you'd asked me any other time, I'd say yes. But I'm enjoying myself."

"Even if you're stuck here?"

Ah, now I realized what he meant. The word *stuck* made it sound like a bad thing. And it really wasn't a bad thing.

I shook my head. "No, I didn't mean it that way. I should've worded it better, like will we be leaving soon or staying longer."

"Yeah, that's a better way of saying it."

One of the dogs darted through the trees and

stopped not far from us. The attention of the rest of the dogs was also on something we couldn't see.

"What?" I whispered and tightened my grip on Barrett's arm.

"I don't know. Could be a squirrel, a bird, grouse, anything."

He certainly didn't seem worried, but it was hard for me not to let an element of alarm creep into my blood.

"A bear?"

"Could be. We just have to be alert." He kept walking, and his calmness made it easy to let myself relax. Moments later, he shifted the rifle in his arm and I froze. As did he.

The dogs started to bark. They kicked up a racket and now I wished we had them all on a leash. I called them, bringing out the treats I had in my pockets. "I think we should put them on the leash.

"Probably. It might be tricky since they're all excited about whatever they smell."

We managed to get most of them leashed and corralled.

Only the shepherd and the golden were still off leash; the golden stayed close to me, while the shepherd seemed to be attached to Barrett's side. I was still worried they'd run off.

"Maybe we should start heading back," I suggested

Barrett nodded. "Of course. Anytime you want to head back is fine. If you want to go now, we can go now."

"I do. I'm worried that it could be a wolf or something even worse."

He nodded again, and just as we were about to turn and retrace our steps, a few of the dogs began to growl. This time Barrett gave his full attention to what might be down the trail.

I heard rustling and my mouth dried up. I saw a dark shape beyond some undergrowth and could hear the branches rustling. And it wasn't from the wind.

"Get behind me." Barrett said. He pushed me back and stepped in front of me. I did as he said and clutched the leashes tighter. I peered around him.

"Oh, my God," I whispered when the creature moved out from behind the trees. "It's a bear. What do we do now?" My flight response kicked in and I was ready to dash back to the cabin, the hell with the big, sloppy boots.

"Shush." Barrett lifted the rifle.

"You're not going to shoot it, are you?" Now I was terrified. I couldn't imagine him shooting this bear, any more than I could imagine being chased by it.

"No, it's black bear and he's more afraid of us that we are of him." Barrett's voice was quiet.

"Are you sure?"

"Yep. It's Bart." I could hear a tinge of humor in his voice.

"Bart? You named him Bart?"

"Yep, Bart the bear. He's an old boy. Been around here for years. He's harmless and visits every now and then."

"You have a pet bear?" I heard the squeak in my voice.

He chuckled. "Hardly my pet, but he deserved a name."

The shepherd began to bark, her ears up and eyes trained on the bear. Bart raised his head and looked at us.

I. Was. Terrified.

"Quiet, girl." Barrett rested his hand on her head and she immediately quieted and sat in the snow by his feet. "Go on, Bart, off you go." Barrett yelled and I was shocked to see the bear turn and lumber off.

"See? He's harmless. But you don't want to get too close just in case. Always be on alert when you're in the forest."

"I've learned a lot since yesterday. But can we please go back to the cabin and leave this excitement behind us?"

Barrett put his arm around my shoulder and pulled me tight. "Anything you want. Your wish is my command."

I looked up at him with a newfound respect. It

seemed that every moment that went by, I learned something new about him. And I really liked what I was learning, too.

"YOU KNOW WHAT'S WEIRD?" she said. "I feel like I've known you for ages, but yesterday was the first time we met. Doesn't it *feel* like ages?"

He didn't immediately respond as they tramped through the snow.

"You're right. It does."

Her eyes held a mischievous glint and he wondered if she was thinking about their time together earlier that day.

"Especially after last night. Well, this morning." She quickly glanced away but not before he saw a blush staining her cheeks.

"You're blushing. I never would've thought."

Beca brought her hands to her cheeks and looked at him through the hair that blew across her face. "That's not polite." Her voice was low and hard to hear over the rising wind and heavier snow.

He pulled her closer and whispered in her ear, "But I like it."

She giggled and slipped her arm around his waist. "Well, okay then. That makes everything better, right?"

He nodded. "It absolutely does. I think we should get back to the cabin, I don't want us to get caught out in a squall. How about we continue this conversation once inside?"

"I like that plan." She was teasing and he enjoyed the banter.

Barrett called for the dogs who were loose and handed out treats to reward them for being so well-behaved. "Good dogs."

They arrived back at the cabin just as a wall of snow came at them reducing visibility to almost nil.

He pushed open the heavy door and they all fell into the vestibule.

"You must have the weather in your bones to know it was going to come that fast. We could've been lost out there! Could you imagine?" She was excited; he heard it in her voice. "Just...wow."

They hung up their parkas and placed the boots on the mat. She took a towel from the bench and tried to dry off the dogs.

"Don't worry about them. They'll dry soon enough." He shook the snow from his hair. "No, we wouldn't have gotten lost, I know my way and I never go anywhere without a compass. But, you never can be too cautious in the forest."

"That's very mountain man. I'm impressed." And he could tell she meant it.

He'd impressed her and that made him proud.

14

Coming across old Bart on our walk this afternoon had definitely been alarming. But seeing a bear live and up close had also been exhilarating. I shook my head, thinking of everything I'd experienced since beginning the journey north to rescue the dogs.

I felt alive! And in a different way than I'd ever felt before.

I didn't know you could feel like this. Coming from a charmed life, there'd never been anything I needed or wanted for. I closed my eyes. There was a lot I'd taken for granted. This venture north was an attempt to find the new me.

I glanced at Barrett sitting in the chair by the window, next to the fireplace. Beyond the glass, the darkened windows reflected the warmly lit interior of the cabin. This man had become my unexpected partner in crime. I watched him read. He was relaxed, absorbed in the book, his leg crossed and ankle resting on his left knee. He held a bottle of beer between two fingers.

I couldn't recall the last time I'd seen anyone read a book. Mostly, noses were plastered to the screen of some kind of device--cell, iPad, computer.

I was guilty of that too. I wandered over to his bookshelf built in under the stairs and ran my fingers along the spines. When we got here, the lack of connection to the outside world had me on edge, as if I was going through withdrawal. Once we'd managed to get a message out and have Tess updated, the urge to stay connected via my phone waned. I was free of its ties, complications and expectations.

And it felt wonderful.

I pulled a book from the shelf and turned, watching him read filled me with a huge sense of contentment. I couldn't see the title but the book appeared old. Our bellies were full after a nice meal and the dogs were contented after their dinner. It was a relaxing evening and I couldn't be happier.

I found a spot on the sofa next to a light, between two other dogs, and drew in a deep breath. The little ladies were on his lap. I hoped he'd adopt them; they were taken with him and he appeared to be with them, as well. The shepherd had also gravitated to Barrett and lay at his feet, her chin on her paws, eyes closed.

The golden pushed his way into my side, with his paw on my forearm and chin resting on my stomach. He looked up at me with those eyes. Those eyes that I swear burrowed deep into my soul. *Oh, man.* He was definitely coming home with me.

The other dogs were scattered around the cabin, sleeping, and the two beagles were lying back to back in front of the fire.

I had done this.

I had saved these wonderful dogs from uncertainty. With the help of Barrett, of course, and I'd be forever grateful to him.

I sighed.

Barrett raised his eyes. "All right?"

I nodded. "This is cozy, being in here safe and warm, with the doggies so content. It's a great feeling." I pulled the blanket over me and the golden, snuggling down into its warmth.

"Does that mean you're starting to like it here?" Barrett asked.

I smiled at him. "It's not so bad."

He laughed, and its deep resonance filled me, reminding me of our early-morning passion. The ladies lifted their heads and the shepherd sat up. Barrett stood and stoked the fire, and warmth immediately radiated from the hearth.

"What's the plan for the dogs? Do you have homes for them all?" Barrett sat on the couch and pulled my feet onto his lap. Immediately the little ladies jumped off the chair and onto his lap, and turned a few times until they found a comfy spot around my ankles. The shepherd moved to his side, too.

"No. I think I have homes for two. It's something I should've thought about, but my impulsiveness sometimes rules and I do things without getting the big picture." I raised my finger. "However, I have the utmost confidence it will all work out."

"In other words, you might end up with most of them?" He stroked the ladies' heads and they both closed their eyes as if they were in total ecstasy. A feeling I could relate to, having experienced his touch.

"No idea. I'm definitely going to keep this guy." I patted the golden's head. "Tess offered to help and is working on placement. Aside from her, this is my own little venture here. So far. Fingers and paws crossed that we'll get lots of support."

That was when the golden pressed his paw into my arm. I petted him and his eyes closed. "Look at him! He's the best, just like those two ladies sitting on you. They'd be perfect for you." I said hoping to plant a seed. I watched a startled expression on his face and my heart dropped. I guessed that was a no.

Barrett shook his head. "I'd never considered adopting a pet before. My job takes me on the road a lot of the time, and I wouldn't be around often enough." He gazed down at the dogs in his lap and I was sure I saw love take over his face. Maybe with a little encouragement he'd be ready to adopt.

"Well, I believe that pets fit into our lives. I had a dog when I was younger, and it nearly killed me when she died. I vowed never to go through it again, it was so painful and took a long time to get over. Then knowing so many lonely and unwanted dogs spurred me to action. Anyway, we make a place for them and then wonder how we ever lived without them. Those two travel well," I pointed out. "Oh, these wonderful faces. How could anyone not want them and throw them away? It breaks my heart."

Barrett was nodding. "After you place these guys, are you going to do another run?" he asked.

I glanced out the window, thinking. "Do this again? I'd like to, but I suppose it depends on how it all plays out in the end. So far, things haven't turned out as planned." I gave him a smile. He returned it and we were silent for a moment, and I wondered what he was thinking. About us? About the dogs? About what comes next?

"Would you do it again? The angel flight?" I asked him. "Pilot with a plane full of dogs?" Tess and I had been calling it that ever since I'd made this arrangement.

He laughed. "Angel Flight? Is that what you're calling it?" He raised a shoulder. "It's actually a good name, because that what you're doing. Rescuing angels."

"Yes, *we* are." I emphasized the *we*. He'd been critical to the execution of this plan.

Barrett looked down at the shepherd and the lap ladies, then stared at me dead on. "Yes, I'd do it again."

I lifted my coffee mug. "Hear, hear. To the Angel Flight pilot!"

Barrett raised his bottle, giving me a nod. "I guess so."

I felt a change in our dynamic. From being together as contractor and contracted, we'd shifted to something more.

"I like where this is going," I said softly.

"You do, do you?" His smile warmed me.

"Yup. However, I think I should make a rule. In order to be part of Angel Flight, you have to foster or adopt a dog."

"Really? Hmm. And you're taking the golden?"

I nodded.

"I know it wouldn't be easy to do this kind of rescue again," I said. "Tess has been fantastic, but I need more help if I want to make this grow. Plus, where am I going to keep these guys when I get home? There I go again, not thinking it through and being optimistic that it'll all work out. Volunteers are the lifeblood of any charitable organization. They need to be treasured."

"Did I hear *volunteer* in there somewhere?" Barrett asked.

"Yes. Volunteers are worth their weight in gold."

"I bet they are."

"You said you'd do this again., Does that mean you'd consider volunteering? As a pilot?" I asked him, surprised I had the courage to be so blunt.

"We can talk about it if or when you have another rescue."

"I could help with the fuel. Maybe it's your time you could donate?" I had enough trust fund money to be able to handle that. As a matter of fact, maybe my family background of charities and galas could be useful.

"How did you get involved with all this anyway?"

"It's something I just stumbled into. A friend of mine, who I'm trying to recruit as a volunteer, rescued a golden retriever from an organization called Golden Rescue Canada, and I saw everything she had to go through in order to adopt. It was quite an intensive process. And when I saw all the dogs available out there for adoption, it moved me. I ended up on some kind of newsletter chain that talked about these dogs up here. Then when the fire happened and they were all displaced, I knew I had to do something. I just had this driving need to save them. And then you came along." I swept my hand in his direction.

"And then me." He smiled.

"Yes, you. A completely unexpected bonus." I wasn't going to blush! No, I wasn't.

"Definitely." He squeezed my foot gently. "You've never done anything like this before?" he asked me.

I shook my head. "Nope, this is all new to me."

"Interesting. First time for me, too. How come you're afraid of flying?"

I looked at him, surprised. "How did you know I was afraid? I never told you."

"It's not hard to tell when someone doesn't like to fly. When you've flown as long as I have, you recognize it. Did you have a bad experience?"

"I don't know really. I've flown a lot, both commercial and private, and it's just not an experience that ever sat well with me. Maybe it's being stuck up in a metal cigar tube at 40,000 feet with no control and at the mercy of the pilots." I shrugged my shoulders. "And it's certain death if the plane drops out of the sky. Splat."

He chuckled. "Flying is actually very safe."

"So everybody keeps telling me." My eyes

widened and I made a face. "I've been through some scary turbulence."

"As have I. Plus, all the dogs flew like champs. They didn't mind."

"But they have no idea what could happen. I do. They're much better flyers than I could ever be." We both laughed.

"Maybe I could help you get over your fear."

"I'd like that."

15

———————

eca stood. "I'm still a little bit hungry. Are you?"

"I could eat." Barrett smiled and he gave her a rather naughty wink. He liked the silly giggle that bubbled up at the same time.

He followed her to the kitchen. "Wine?" he asked.

"It's getting late, so maybe just a glass." She opened the fridge. "Do you have a secret stash of wine? It's seems like there's a never-ending supply." She closed the refrigerator and moved over to the cupboards

"I keep a good supply of pretty much everything here. In case of power outages, snowstorms, being stranded...you know."

"Actually, yes, I do." She cast him a smile over her shoulder. "Oh, potato chips?" She held them up.

"Fine with me."

Barrett came up behind her as she opened the bag and poured the chips into a bowl. He put the wine bottle on the counter and rested his hands on her hips, then slid them to her belly. He liked how her breath caught when he splayed his fingers and pulled her close.

Her head dropped to the side, inviting him to find that tender spot he'd discovered in the early dawn. She sagged in his arms, a soft sigh escaping her lips.

"This is certainly the last thing I ever expected to happen on a rescue mission," she murmured.

"You and me both." He spun her around, looked into her passion- filled eyes and hoped there'd continue to be tons of snow so they could stay here and be together. He didn't bother to process the thought and what it meant

She reached for him and tugged his head down until their lips met. He couldn't breathe or think; it was purely about sensation. The pressure of his hands on her back locked them together.

This seemed perfectly right. How was it possible he felt as if he'd known her a lifetime?

He wanted her.

Not just physically either.

He hadn't realized how empty the cabin had been all these years. He'd built it for himself, and it was home. He'd never questioned his solitary life before, but meeting Beca through their video-chats and then finally meeting her in person had opened his eyes. He wanted to share his life, his home, his world with someone.

He'd met lots of people in his line of work, but he'd never met anyone like her. It took a special person to adapt and live in the wilderness. Even with all the comforts and conveniences he'd built into the cabin.

Just in case there was a person he grew to care for, someone he wanted to bring here.

Beca hadn't complained about anything. Yet. However, she was a city girl, and from their conversations and her freedom with money, he suspected she came from a wealthy background. Used to a life of luxury, parties, glitz and glamor.

None of which could be found within hours of his cabin.

But now, with his arms around Beca, holding her close, he actually felt light-headed with happiness. She held him in return and fit to him seamlessly. Still, he was cautious about letting his emotions get the better of him. She'd leave, with all her dogs, and that would be that.

She lifted her head, and he studied her face,

memorizing the color of her eyes, the curl of her lashes, the arched wing of her brows, her soft skin and her lips. She pulled him down again and he slanted his mouth over hers, sweeping his tongue along her lips until she opened them.

Her kisses inflamed him. She didn't hold back her passion and swept him up in the vortex. Their tongues met, and he breathed her in, knowing he'd never forget her scent.

He ran his hands down her back, cupped her bottom and lifted her onto the counter. Then he nudged himself between her knees and when she wrapped her legs around his hips, he braced himself against the counter. It was all he could do to stay standing.

"Oh, Barrett." Her sigh against his mouth, with his name on her lips, ignited a fire inside him.

He was falling for her. And her reactions toward him said she was feeling the same. It was all so sudden it seemed surreal. He tightened his hold on her, deepening the kiss until everything around him faded away, and all his senses were entirely focused on Beca.

Clarity returned when a dog jumped up and placed his paws on Barrett's back, knocking him off balance.

"Wha—?" He caught himself before stumbling forward into Beca. "Hey, doggo, not cool." The big

Heinz 57 mix of a dog rested his chin on Barrett's shoulder, panting and tongue lolling. "Okay, down, boy."

The dog pranced and did a little dance, and soon the others came into the kitchen to see what the commotion was all about.

"Oh, the joy of pets." She laughed. "They have a way of breaking up the moment."

"That they do. He's kind of a cool dog, though." Barrett helped her off the counter, disappointed by the interruption.

Beca took his hand and pulled him closer, and with her other hand reached up to cup his cheek. She looked deep into his eyes, and emotion tightened in his chest. He liked this woman. A lot.

"Thank you," she said softly.

He furrowed his brows. "For what?"

"For understanding, for going with this crazy change of circumstances, for helping me with the dogs. F-for everything. I'm glad we got to know each other before yesterday with our chats and video calls. And I'm so glad we know each other even better now," She paused. "Also, thank you for...being safe. For keeping me safe, I'm not sure how to explain it, but I don't feel any harm will come to me when I'm with you."

He smiled. Her words meant a lot and he actually choked up. He had a multitude of things he could say, but he was cautious, suddenly feeling vulnerable.

"You're welcome," he finally managed. "This has certainly been a different kind of job. I like how it turned out. And maybe after this, there'll be more we can do to get to know each other."

She nodded and her smile warmed him. "I was thinking the same thing."

He kissed her tenderly until another couple of dogs pushed their way between them.

"Dogs! What a way to interrupt," Barrett said to the pups staring up at them with big soft eyes. He reached down and petted a smooth head.

His stomach growled and the dogs barked. "They might be as hungry as I am."

"Well, then, let's get cracking." Beca carried the bowl of chips to the table in front of the fire, dogs at her heels. "The wine's your job and I'll fill the dog bowls."

"Yes, ma'am."

A short while later, he pulled Beca down beside him, the chip bowl handy. She'd found a DVD and they were about to watch it.

"I can't believe you like *Alien*." He shook his head and took a handful of chips.

"Why? It's a great movie."

"You constantly surprise me Beca."

"Good."

16

The next morning after cooking bacon, eggs and hash browns, which were delicious, we ventured out with the dogs.

The snow was still heavy and the sky was dark. I was feeling much more comfortable here and actually welcomed the walk to the hangar. We needed the other bag of dog food I'd brought.

I had treats in my pocket and we decided to let the dogs run. They didn't really go far, except for the beagles when they picked up a scent. The husky went off, too. We could still see them and when I called, they came for their treats.

"Let's take a look at the runway," Barrett suggested and we followed him. The dogs having fun and romping in the snow off leash, was a far cry from the way they were when we collected them the other day. Had it really only been two days ago? It was hard to believe.

We walked past the hangar to a stretch of land that was bare of trees.

"Wow, you can hardly tell it's there," I said, pointing back at the hangar. The snow had to be almost hip-high and there were even deeper drifts where the wind had swirled out of the trees alongside the runway.

"Yeah, it'll definitely take a while to clear once this lets up." He crossed his arms, gazing at the monumental task in front of us. "I'm half-debating getting a head start on it."

My shoulders drooped. "Does that meant we're leaving soon?"

Barrett turned with a wide smile on his face. "Why, I think I heard disappointment in your tone. Don't want to go?"

I shrugged. "I'm not sure. Maybe, yes. Maybe no. I like it here!" The words rushed out of me and we stood in the silence, snow falling around us. "How long would it take for the snow to melt?"

Barrett laughed and pulled me in for a hug. "Those words just made my day. And a while for the snow to melt."

I wrapped my arms around his waist and held tight. No, I wasn't ready to go back to the world yet.

"Come on. Let's get that bag of food. I want to show you something."

We called the dogs, got the food and took it back to the cabin.

"What did you want to show me?" I asked, super-curious.

"We'll go around this way." He took my hand and led me through the trees, in the opposite direction from the cabin.

A short hike later, he stopped and told me to listen.

I pushed the hood back from my ears to hear better and watched Barrett. "Water rushing?"

"Yes, just along here."

We emerged from the trees and I gasped. The dogs fanned out, sniffing. We were on a flat rock jutting out into the lake. In front of us to the left was a waterfall. It appeared to come pooling down the rocky, pine-covered slope. Fantastical ice formations edged the rocks from the water spray.

"It's spectacular!"

"I thought you'd like it. My place is around the bend to the right, on a bay off the main lake." Barrett pointed across the lake and swept his hand past the falls. "It's wonderful here in the summer. It can be a little buggy in the spring, but well worth it."

"I can imagine. I noticed the lake when we were

landing the other day. Does anyone else live on the lake?"

He shook his head. "No, this side is my land and across there is Crown land."

"Wow, you own a lake!"

"Well, maybe half a lake. Really, nature owns the lake. I just like to think of myself as a custodian."

I turned to him. What an interesting thing to say. He looked out over the frozen water with the most serene expression on his face.

He really was at home here. I followed his gaze. Could I be at home here, in the middle of nowhere? Could he be at home in the city?

I glanced down at our hands, fingers still entwined. My stomach felt heavy.

"If only..." I whispered.

"If only what?" he asked.

"Oh, nothing, just daydreaming." There was no point thinking of *what ifs* and *if onlys*. We had different lives. Different obligations. I couldn't see a way to unite them to give us even a chance at creating something together.

The mood shifted and I was sad. We walked back to the cabin in silence, and I was pleased the dogs followed us without having to be called or offered treats. Back inside, the little old ladies--we'd left them behind--greeted us with little yips from the blanket they'd nested in on the chair by the window.

We were silent, lost in our own thoughts. It was as if we were on either side of a chasm. Could still see each other, but not touch, connect or be close.

After our lunch, I picked up the book I'd started to read, it was about exploration in the Canadian North, and sat by the fire reading. I glanced out the window at the few dogs outside. I watched them play and I was filled with happiness. Then on the heels of that, tears prickled my eyes. For crying out loud! Why did I feel teary?

I was the optimist, right? Always finding the silver lining. This time I was having a hard time finding it.

Barrett was in his office, the shepherd with him. The golden was lying on my feet, sleeping. Every now and then, he'd let out little yips and growls. He was dreaming. I smiled and watched his nose twitch, and his paws moved as if he was in a great battle.

I put the book down, unable to concentrate, and lifted the mug of hot chocolate. I suddenly remembered the paperwork given to me when I met the coordinator of the shelter the dogs came from. I should go through it.

I rose, the golden following me, and pulled out a chair at the oak table. He lay at my feet again.

I opened the file. The first page was about him. He was four and a half, and had recently been neutered; he'd had all his shots and his name was Milo. I gazed down at him and I knew I was going to keep him. No way could I part with him after bonding these few days.

"You're not a Milo. What could I call you?" Those wonderful eyes gazed up at me. "I know! Hiro. You'll be my Hiro. Is that okay with you?" I whispered. He heard me, and his tail swayed back and forth. I was impressed by the intelligence reflected in those expressive eyes and stretched my hand to him. He licked me gently, sighed and rested his head back on my feet.

"I'd take that as a yes." Barrett came in from his office.

"Me, too." I flipped through the folder. "Oh, wow, the beagles are Zelda and Fitzgerald, how cute is that!" I flipped a page and I pointed at the shepherd beside Barrett. "I think that one loves you. Her name is Kylie and ... oh! She's a trained security dog. Imagine that."

"I thought she had training. She's well-mannered and was very alert when we went for the food." He petted her and she sat beside him, her eyes half closed.

"You'll adopt her, right." I said, and it wasn't a question.

He glanced at me. "Actually, I was thinking of the two little ladies there." They were on the sofa, cuddled close. As if they knew he was talking about them, they raised their heads with interest.

"Oh, that would be fantastic!" Happiness chased away the sadness I'd been feeling only moments before. "But you can't not take Kylie. She's in love with you."

When we went our separate ways, we would always have the link of the dogs.

"I'm definitely bring Hiro home." I pointed to my feet.

"Ah, yes. He seems to have adopted you," Barrett commented. "Do you think you'll have trouble finding homes for the rest?

"I have no idea. I was originally supposed to have only five, which seemed enough of a challenge to rehome. But eleven?"

"Maybe you'll keep them all."

I gazed around the room at the sleeping pups, then rose to look out the window at the bigger ones outside. Now covered in snow. A couple of them stood at the door, while the husky was lying down with his nose in the air.

"I don't know if I could handle more than one—or maybe two," I said when I opened the door, almost bowled over by the incoming dogs.

"Hey, you," I called to the husky. "Are you coming in or staying there?"

He looked at me, then raised his face to the snow again. Total indifference.

"Yeah, I think he's staying where he is. By the way, we finally have cell service and Wi-Fi. I thought you'd want to know."

I was about to jump up and get my phone. Something stopped me. "That's great."

"You don't sound very excited. I thought you'd be burning the airwaves as soon as you could."

"Yeah, me too." The strangest feeling enveloped me. I realized I didn't feel stranded anymore. Instead, I felt a sense of comfort, home, contentment.

The thought of calling the outside world didn't sit right. First, I was worried about Barrett plowing the runway. And now I didn't want to make any phone calls. Or even check to see what messages I had.

It was an intrusion into our world. And I didn't like it one bit.

I walked back to the window and watched the husky in his element out in the makeshift yard, protected by the fencing Barrett had put up. When I thought of all the things he'd done over the last few days, and our growing passion, I had a sudden revelation. I didn't want it to be over.

But what about him? What did *he* want? We'd

never ventured so far as to discuss the after-blizzard possibilities.

Leaving here would mean going back to a life with family pressures that frustrated the heck out of me. Having to make explanations once again to parents despite being thirty-one years old. And I simply couldn't face it anymore. I'd met my share of family obligations; now it was my turn to live my life. Find out about *me,* who I am, and step out on my own journey. But if I didn't go back, then what about the possibility of future rescues?

Which had begun on a flight with Barrett Kingston, bush pilot extraordinaire.

Heat flushed my face as I thought of our intimate moments together. I wasn't the sort to have one- night stands or pick up guys in a bar, even if it could be exciting. So, it was rather uncharacteristic that I'd basically fallen into Barrett's arms. But, oh, those arms!

All of that excitement, that passion, would come to an end.

I let out a big sigh, still gazing out the window into the blowing snow.

"What's up?" Barrett came in behind me and slid his arm around my shoulder. He nuzzled my hair. "I know something's bothering you. Why not get it off your chest?"

I wasn't quite sure what to tell him. If I expressed how I felt about leaving him and staying here, wouldn't that put him on the spot? We hadn't discussed what might happen. Originally the intention was to go our separate ways. After all, the job would be completed. He would have fulfilled his contract and be on to the next one. I'd be finding homes for these dogs and looking for another venture to get tangled up in rescuing dogs.

"I'm not sure you'd understand," I finally said.

"Why don't you try me?"

I drew in a breath and held it for a beat. "With Wi-Fi working and when you mentioned plowing earlier, I realized all this-" I flicked my hand at the room behind us "-is going to end. And that reminds me of my life beyond here." I turned to look at him. "It means back to civilization. Back to work. Back to jobs. Back to all the worries and away from you—"

"Whoa, whoa. Hold on there. I think you're getting ahead of yourself." He lifted my chin with his finger.

"What you mean? All of that's waiting for me. Out there."

"I think you're jumping the gun here. Have you looked outside?"

"Of course." I turned and looked out the window again and then at Barrett.

"Snow's still coming down," he said. "And the

wind's still high. We're not going anywhere for at least a day or two. Possibly longer.

I searched his eyes, looking for emotion, feelings, anything that might tell me how he felt.

"And you know what? You don't have to go if you want to stay longer." His voice had lowered to a soft and intimate tone that surrounded me like a comfy blanket.

A million questions just about tumbled out of my mouth. He pressed his fingers to my lips.

"You don't have to decide right now. You have a couple of days at least. I think we can make the most of it, don't you?" He held the side of my face with his palm.

"What do *you* want?" I asked.

"I want what you want."

I shook my head. "No, don't do that. I need an answer. A real answer."

"Beca, don't wind yourself up for no reason. I *do* want what you want. I want you to choose without pressure from me. I would never want to sway you to do what I want. And I wouldn't want you to do that to me, either."

"But Barrett, I've loved being here with you. I want to stay. I don't want to leave. I can't bear the thought of us being apart." I paused for a second or two. "I don't understand how I could have such powerful feelings so quickly."

He lifted my face and placed a gentle kiss on my lips. "I understand how you feel."

He looked into my eyes and I could have melted into his arms. "You do?"

He smiled and nodded. "I do."

"So, we have the next few days to figure it out." I drew in a ragged breath.

"Yes, figure out how we'll make it work between us."

"Oh, Barrett. I've been going around and around this in my mind, wondering *if* our lives could blend."

"We'll never know unless we try," he murmured against my hair. "But I do think you should make contact with Tess and advise her you'll be here for at least a few more days. And that the dogs are safe and everything's fine. Then we can block out the world again and it'll be just the two of us alone in the wilderness." He pulled me into his arms, and I laced my fingers behind his neck.

"And the dogs." I smiled up at him.

"Yes, and the dogs."

He lowered his head. We kissed, with our dogs gathered around our legs. And, I didn't want to be anywhere else in the world, except right here. In the wild with my bush pilot.

And our dogs.

·　·　·

I HOPE YOU ENJOYED BECA & Barrett's story. When things don't go to plan the outcome can be so unexpected and exciting. Start your journey with Chet and Jenna, HERE and watch their plans go awry in the face of Mother Nature's wrath in PASSION COWBOY STYLE

Receive a complimentary copy of MY READING JOURNAL, book tracker when you sign up for my **NEWSLETTER**

To help other readers discover books you enjoy, while supporting authors, please leave honest reviews.

MORE BOOKS!

Shana Gray writes contemporary romance and women's fiction that just might make you laugh. When she's not writing, she can be found daydreaming about life, and making travel plans to far off lands to feed her wanderlust.

Join Shana's Shananigators Facebook Group

Single Title

Working Girl

Backdraft

Public Displays of Affection

Northern Rescue

The Road Home

Summer With a Billionaire

Girls Weekend Away Series

What Happens in Vegas – Free eBook

Meet Me in San Francisco

The Nashville Bet

A Match Made in Monaco

Harlequin Blaze

A Cowboy in Paradise

More than a Fling

For TV, movie & foreign rights, Shana is represented by

Louise Fury

5676 Riverdale Ave, Suite 101, Riverdale, NY 10471

917-545-2603. https://www.thefuryagency.com/

9 781738 348060